LOVE UNLOCKED

By

LIBBY WATERFORD

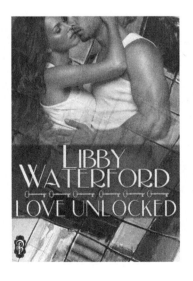

Decadent Publishing Company, LLC
www.decadentpublishing.com

This book is a work of fiction. Names, characters, places, and incidents are the products of the author's imagination or used fictitiously. Any resemblance to actual events, locales or persons, living or dead, is entirely coincidental.

Love Unlocked
Copyright 2015 by Libby Waterford
ISBN: 978-1-61333-816-2
Cover art by Tibbs Designs

All rights reserved. Except for use in any review, the reproduction or utilization of this work, in whole or in part, in any form by any electronic, mechanical or other means now known or hereafter invented, is forbidden without the written permission of the publisher.

Published by Decadent Publishing Company
www.decadentpublishing.com

Printed in the United States of America

~Dedication~

For Dylan

Chapter One

*E*ve Caplin was used to being on the wrong side of a locked door. Until recently, her livelihood had depended on her ability to get past any lock to reach whatever treasure lay on the other side. She always succeeded. Thus, her irritation at being locked out of her brand new house—unable to let herself in by means traditional or otherwise—threatened to swamp her sunny mood. Not exactly an auspicious beginning to home ownership.

Her lock picks were in a safe deposit box in San Francisco. She could probably break a window, but she couldn't bear to do damage to the beautiful house she'd only taken possession of half an hour before. Even though her nearest neighbor was a quarter mile down the road, out of sight, she didn't want to announce her presence to the area by being seen shinnying up a drainpipe in her snakeskin Ferragamo flats. Besides, all of that illicit behavior was part of a life she was trying to leave behind.

The irony of having to call a locksmith tempered her almost tearful happiness at the second chance this Victorian-style house perched on top of Oak Grove Hill represented. Waiting on the flagstone front step gave her time to daydream about paint colors and furniture configurations, and she was so occupied with tapping to-do lists into her sleek little phone that she started at the crunch of tires on the gravel driveway. *Her* driveway. The thought made her smile, despite her idiotic lapse with the house keys.

Then the locksmith swung out of his sparkling clean truck, headed straight for her, and all thoughts of paint, sofas, and misplaced keys melted out of her brain.

Her first impression was raw strength. His shoulders were powerful, and his arms filled out the sleeves of his plain white tee. She'd never met him, but the contradictory features of his fascinatingly masculine face were familiar somehow. Strong nose, full lips, dark slanted eyes—all shockingly appealing. He could have been the model for a Michelangelo sculpture, a Renaissance hunk carved out of caramel-colored marble. If she'd met him last week when she'd still called Paris home, she would have assumed he was Italian, but since they were smack in the middle of California's coastline, his Mediterranean looks probably meant he had Latino heritage.

"Locked out?" he said in a smooth bass.

"Yes." She rose to let him by, but didn't move quickly enough to avoid his elbow brushing against her as he set his toolbox on the step. The brief touch made her shiver. *Get it together, Eve.* There was no cause to become so unsettled by one beautiful man.

"This will only take a minute," he said, all professional seriousness.

"Super."

He knelt and applied his tool to the lock. He knew what he was doing, but he was slow. It would have taken her about fifteen seconds to do what was taking him two minutes. She curbed her impatience and took the opportunity to study him.

Glossy brown hair curled around his ears, and the hands working the lock were strong and agile. They could have been a pianist's hands. She liked the combination of his wide mouth with its lush bottom lip made for sin, and his eyes, dark and hooded with concentration.

What could he do if he applied that concentration and those hands to some of her less accessible places?

Hold it. That was the last thing she needed at the moment. Not to mention how a man that attractive, with no wedding ring, was the definition of dangerous to a woman whose number one priority was keeping a low profile. Unless he was gay. A girl could hope.

"What's your name?" she asked as the door swung open.

He looked her in the eye and the realization struck her why he seemed familiar. She knew who he was.

"Hudson," he said. "That'll be thirty-nine bucks."

"Hudson," she repeated. "I'm Eve."

He already knew that from the message given to him by the answering service. What the lady who routed Triple A Locksmith's calls hadn't said was that Eve Caplin would be a knockout brunette, as petite as a gymnast, but with twice the curves. Something told him they were dangerous curves. Hudson found an invoice and got busy writing, the faster to get out of her way.

His concentration had been shot since he'd arrived and felt her watching him. He'd tried to keep his eyes on the job, but he wanted to look over and drink in more of her cool, creamy skin and the thick black hair drawn away from her face in a loose knot. How far would it fall down her back if he pulled it free? He found himself needing to know. Acknowledging the desire made him wary.

"We haven't met, but I think I know your work," she said, in a soft but commanding voice that had his body snapping to attention.

Hudson stopped filling out the invoice and regarded his customer carefully. Her eyes were green, like the jade that covered some of the beaches farther north. He had the sudden urge to sketch her. He'd need to use a delicate touch as her features, though striking, were also somehow effervescent, changing as she adjusted the tilt of her head, or lowered sooty lashes over those alluring eyes. The idea stuck in his brain like a burr. It had been a long time since he'd wanted to sketch anything, let alone a woman.

She peered at him as if she expected him to say something. When he didn't, she added, "Do you want to come in?"

Hudson shrugged and followed her into the front hallway. He only wanted to get out of the late afternoon sun, not prolong his contact with this seductive creature. Just one glance told him the entire space was as empty as Chelsea Creek in August. Eve took a left through what was probably destined to be the living room into a big, open kitchen. A set of shiny keys sat on a gray marble countertop, beside a bottle of California sparkling wine adorned with a gift tag that proclaimed "Welcome Home! From Chelsea Realty".

Eve scooped up the keys and dropped them in the pocket of her oversized red cardigan. "I was so excited to move in my one box of stuff that I left my keys inside." She gestured to the bottle of wine. "No ice, no fridge, no glasses. I guess the bubbly will have to wait."

"Too bad."

"Yes, it is. I can't think of a time when I've wanted to celebrate more."

"Oh, I open doors all the time," he said dryly. Then he shook his head. Why was he bantering with her?

She smiled a little. "I meant buying my first house. Though, champagne is always a good idea, so I guess it will keep."

Her enthusiasm was kind of sweet.

"I do have a bottle of water, if you're thirsty."

"No, thanks." It had been a while since he'd worked a shift for Triple A Locksmith, but he remembered the drill. You let them in, you got your thirty-nine bucks, you left. No champagne or water. No banter. But this small, jade-eyed woman intrigued him. Her empty house intrigued him. The fact that she said she knew his work aroused his curiosity even more.

"You're Hudson Cleary, aren't you?" she said, following up on that very topic.

He hesitated. "Guilty."

"I thought so. A friend of mine has one of your Provence

series in his home. It's stunning."

His astonishment at being recognized was dwarfed by his consternation at her compliment. He managed, "Thanks," but she started talking again before he'd finished spitting out the word.

"But what...."

"What am I doing moonlighting as a locksmith?" he supplied. He didn't blame her for wondering. He was pondering what a gorgeous woman with a friend who owned one of his earliest and most expensive paintings, who recognized a semi-obscure painter by sight, was doing on the middle-of-nowhere Central California coast.

"Well, yes."

His recent self-imposed exile had left him short on social niceties. "I'm filling in for a friend," he said brusquely.

Her raised eyebrows invited him to continue, so he forced himself to elaborate. "This was my father's business. Now it's my brother's. He and his wife are out of town, so I told them I'd mind the store. I used to work summers with my dad."

"Before you became an internationally famous painter," she said, seemingly amused at the unlikely origin story.

"Before that," he agreed, the gruffness slowly leaving his voice. She had managed to loosen him up a bit, but the pause that followed reminded him they were here to finish their business.

He handed her the invoice. She counted out exactly thirty-nine dollars from her designer shoulder bag.

"Do you think your brother could do some additional work for me when he has some time? I'd like to change the locks and a few other things. Does he do security systems?"

He had to remind himself not to be disappointed by her return to business. "Sure. I'll have him call you to set up an appointment."

"Thanks."

He picked up his tools. "I assume you just moved in."

"Well, I can't claim to have moved in, but I did take

ownership this morning. I was so excited I locked myself out."

"New to the area?"

She paused a slight second. "Yes. I don't suppose you could recommend a hotel nearby? I'm not going to be able to stay here until I get a bed."

The last word conjured a flash of heat in his belly. He imagined her lying naked in his heavy four-poster, and he cleared his throat. "Well, the Chelsea Inn is basic but clean. Left, off the 1."

"Lovely. I'll give that a go."

Her speech had a European flavor and her American accent was overlaid with a veneer of British poshness, adding another dimension to her appeal and another puzzle to the stack.

"Thanks again," she said.

Though she was clearly dismissing him, Hudson lingered. He wanted to know why this woman's face made him itch for a pencil and paper when he hadn't touched either in nearly two years.

He hovered by the door. "Who are you?" he asked before he could stop himself.

She laughed, a smooth, sophisticated chortle that seemed a little forced. "I'm an out-of-towner looking for a fresh start. Good enough?"

"Fresh," he repeated, as if that was the only word she'd said. He deliberately ran his gaze up and down her body. She was as refreshing as a breeze kicking off the Pacific to cool a sweltering summer day. He hadn't known he'd been craving a change in the weather but now that a mysterious, sexy stranger had raised his internal thermostat a few degrees, he could stand to cool down a little.

Eve didn't seem offended by his appraisal. She was so beautiful she was probably used to being looked at, complimented, commented upon.

"Nice to meet you," she said.

He allowed himself to be pushed out the door, enjoying the feel of her hand steering him past the threshold. She followed him out, and, to his surprise, shut the door behind them.

"Are you headed back to town? Would you mind if I followed you to the hotel you mentioned?"

"Not at all." She was practical, he had to give her that. He hoped he hadn't made her too uncomfortable. "And I'll ask my brother to call you."

"I appreciate that."

He pulled himself away from her humming energy and climbed into the truck. He drove carefully down the hill, watching her gray compact in the rearview mirror. A part of him felt oddly cut off when she turned into the hotel's parking lot and he lost sight of her. He traced the outline of her face on the steering wheel, hoping to keep the lines in his muscle memory until he could get home to his studio. He'd start in charcoal.

Chapter Two

*A*mazing what you could do with a wallet full of cash and some liberal smiling. Eve had braced herself to spend as much as a week at the Chelsea Inn, but three days later found herself checking out. She was on her way to her house on the hill to meet a moving truck full of appliances and her brand new, California King-size bed.

She was also meeting Will Cleary, locksmith and security expert, or so his website claimed. She'd checked both Cleary men out on her phone's tiny browser while trying to take a bubble bath in the too-small hotel tub. There wasn't much on Will, but Triple A Locksmith had positive online reviews, and she didn't see a reason not to use him for the work she needed done.

Hudson Cleary had a far wider Internet presence, with articles written about him in major newspapers and art magazines, as well as a professional website showcasing his work. His paintings were owned by a dozen major museums, but he hadn't had a show in over two years. Nothing on his website seemed recent.

Hudson had come onto the scene as a precocious college dropout, having been taken under the wing of one of the West Coast's biggest gallery owners, who'd given him his own show at the tender age of twenty-two. His extraordinary work had propelled him from wunderkind to top-of-the-heap contemporary artist, a position he'd held for a decade before all but disappearing two years ago.

What was he up to here in tiny Chelsea? Even with her research skills, she found little information online about his personal life; he almost qualified for the "reclusive genius" label. She could have queried her contacts at some of the galleries he'd shown at, but that would have been crossing the line from idle curiosity to stalker behavior. The most she could figure was that since his last show, prices for his paintings had reached a point where even with her generous collecting hand, she'd have to think twice about investing in one of his pieces. And since she no longer acquired works of art unless she paid for them, she'd simply have to get by without a Hudson Cleary abstract.

Her thoughts turned to the crate of paintings slowly wending its way from Europe. She hoped they'd arrive soon, as she worried over them the way a mother might fret over a child gone to sleep away camp. When it arrived, the artwork she'd painstakingly collected over the last decade would make this new place she'd chosen feel like home.

As she let herself into her house, her sigh turned into a yawn. Outfitting a house from scratch was exhausting, and there was still so much to be done. Her next priority was replacing her tin can rental car with something more substantial. A utilitarian sedan would strike the right note for her new surroundings. A shame she'd had to leave her sporty Aston Martin behind when she left Paris, but the cash from that sale and her savings had so far been enough to finance her California reinvention.

Her tiredness was forgotten when she found that the fridge delivered yesterday was humming and already ice cold. Pathetic how enjoyable the simple act of unloading a few bags of groceries into it was. She shoved the crisper drawer closed—she may have overdone it on the greens—as a knock came at the door. Will Cleary.

Unless they were identical twins, Hudson stood on her front step, not Will. "This is a surprise."

"Hi. Will got held up. He asked me to do a walkthrough with you, take some notes so he can get started on parts orders."

"A few of the things I want are kind of complicated." She afforded herself the luxury of taking in his well-built frame from his broad shoulders straining a gray and blue flannel shirt, his finely muscled forearms, to promisingly large boot-clad feet. A pencil was lodged behind his right ear. He had a notebook in his left hand, and a bulge in his pocket, probably a cell phone. She could find some of his other bulges if she went looking, which she definitely did not plan to do. "Are you up for it?"

"Try me."

His posture was as casual as the day she'd first met him, but she noticed the masculine energy that seemed to thrum and match the pulse of the blood pumping hot through her body. To ground herself, she tried to focus on the work at hand.

"Okay, let's start right here. I need a new deadbolt and lock for the front door. Something really strong and smooth, nothing cheap. I absolutely hate wrestling with a sticky key to get in my own front door."

Hudson tugged the pencil from behind his ear and started scribbling. Eve had to drag her gaze from his nimble fingers to the list she'd entered in her smartphone.

"I'd also like a keypad entry system wired to all the doors and windows. If so much as a bird flies into a window mistakenly, I want the system to go off."

"So something sensitive." He didn't take his eyes off his notebook.

Eve was chagrined that he didn't seem to feel the electric current running between them. She should have been relieved.

"Yes, something along the lines of a Lorex. At my last gallery, we had a system custom designed, but I don't have time for that."

"You worked at a gallery?"

He glanced up from his notes, ignoring, as usual, whatever she'd said that didn't appear to interest him. If it would get this done faster, she would tell him what he wanted to know.

"Yes, most recently I was assistant curator at Bonard's in Paris. Before that, at their sister galleries in London and Vienna."

Hudson's eyebrows rose. "What do you expect to do out here? Chelsea has one gallery. Mostly seagulls and sunsets."

Was it a mistake to have told him? She'd forgotten for a moment that he had connections to the world she had left behind. Perhaps it was a good thing he was focused more on her resume than on her knowledge of security systems.

"I'm reinventing myself." She shrugged. He wasn't the only one who could be terse.

He quirked his mouth at her answer and turned his attention back to his notes. "So you want a system that will alert the cops. I have to warn you, in a rural area like this, you aren't going to get a real fast response time."

"Are there any local security companies? One with patrol cars or anything like that?"

Hudson's mouth flattened into a thin line. "Not that I know of. My brother might be willing to subcontract the work out...if you really think it's necessary. B&Es are pretty rare in these parts."

If her home was broken into, it wouldn't be an amateur looking for electronics and jewelry. It would be a professional, and this system would be the first line of defense. She had a few other tricks up her sleeve.

"I'm cautious," she said crisply. "Moving on."

They covered the downstairs at a brisk pace, but if she was trying to overwhelm him, he'd show her he could keep up. She had made progress in the last few days. Simple but costly looking furniture had appeared in the living room, while stainless steel appliances filled out the kitchen, and items like a simple glass bowl brimming with fruit and placed on the kitchen's long marble counter added a homey touch.

She rattled off some more specifications, then led him upstairs so he could count the windows and take some measurements. His pencil rarely stopped moving on the page. When they arrived at the landing to go down again, she stopped.

"Are you writing a novel?" she asked in that faintly accented voice of hers.

He wanted to grin but held back. He stilled his writing hand and flipped the notebook around so she could see his careful notations of everything she'd said, plus a remarkably accurate drawing of her face, done in bold lines with rough shading for depth.

"You just drew that?" she asked.

"Yeah." He didn't tell her he'd sketched her from memory half a dozen times over the last few days, but that he'd needed to see her again to capture the precise line of her chin.

Surprise, irritation, and appreciation clashed for dominance on her face.

"It's lovely," she said.

"So are you."

Her mouth opened and closed a few times, then she frowned as if dismayed by her lack of a witty response, which made him like her even more. His heart sped up and he heard nothing but the rhythm of his blood, saw nothing but the blush stealing over her porcelain cheekbones.

They stood side by side at the top of the stairs, as if descending would end a moment neither wanted to break. Now was the time to act. He touched her arm, keeping her on the landing with him. She stared up at him, a foot shorter and dainty in some kind of flouncy flat shoes.

"Would you...."

Eve leaned her head to the side, waiting for him to finish, her lips slightly parted. Why was this so difficult? His hands started to sweat, something they hadn't done since his date with Lorraine Strong at the homecoming dance senior year. What he was about to ask was an enormous step forward into unforeseen territory. He had to take this risk. That's what artists did, and he was still an artist, despite not having created art in two years.

"Would you be willing to do a sitting for me? An hour or two, here or at my studio, whatever you're comfortable with?" He spoke quickly, the faster to have the question asked and out there.

As much as he wanted to explore this flash of inspiration she'd managed to spark in him, a part of him wanted her to say no. Then he could ask her on a proper date. He didn't have much experience working with live models, since he had been an abstract painter inspired by landscapes, but he'd heard enough horror stories from his artist friends to know you never, ever slept with your models, at least while you were painting them. It got too complicated, blurring the lines of professionalism that serious painters kept well established. He had the sense that if he showed interest in Eve Caplin, the woman, she'd never consent to sit for him. He might never get the courage to try to paint again if he let this tender bud of progress wither and die. As interested as he might be in her personally, he had to sate his interest in her as an artist first.

"You want to paint me?" She paused, and Hudson sensed something shift as her smile hardened into something merely polite, and her words took on a superficial tone. "How flattering. I'm afraid, however, that I am drowning in work to get moved in here, and I can't spare the time."

Her words made him oddly angry. He knew what he was asking was an imposition, but he needed her. He'd seen a softer side to her, but here she was, giving him the polished version of herself that he didn't buy.

If she wanted to play it cool, he could play it frosty. "Of course, I understand. Think nothing of it." His voice dripped with icicles.

She practically floated down the stairs, back straight as an arrow, her long, graceful fingers trailing lightly over the stair rail. Hudson thrust the pencil behind his ear and slammed his notebook closed, following her with loudly clomping footsteps. The doorbell rang as her cellphone went off. Eve answered both while thanking him coolly for his time.

"Don't worry, I won't bother you again," he said, and gladly left her to the cable guy.

Chapter Three

*E*ve bolted upright in bed. Early morning gray light filtered through a break in her new charcoal-toned blackout curtains. She preferred a pitch-black room to sleep in, but that sliver of light wasn't what had woken her up. She'd been running in her dream, chased by a faceless demon, never able to approach a haven of light that flickered on the edge of her consciousness. She couldn't breathe, couldn't run fast enough. He was going to catch up with her before she reached the safety of the light.

She forced herself to take several deep breaths. She was awake; the dream was over. She ignored the shivers that were slowly subsiding and got up quickly. A hot shower and a cup of coffee would clear away the remnants of the dream, and the cloud of sadness that followed. Eve paused to pull the covers up. Her petite frame barely made a dent in the oversized bed, a visual reminder of her solitary existence.

For years, she'd lived in cities, among crowds, with flat mates and housemates. For a time, she'd even lived in a hotel, constantly surrounded by other guests and the staff. It had seemed safer to live anonymously amongst people who could distract you from things you'd rather not think about.

When that life had become more hazardous than she'd bargained for, it hadn't taken much to let go. She said goodbye to beautiful European locales, her demanding work at the gallery, her lucrative extracurricular activities, and retreated to this house on a hill. By removing herself from the scene in which she'd occupied an important but precarious niche, she'd avoided the immediate risks. It would have been smart to shed her name, as well. But she hadn't had time to set up a new identity for herself. Officially, Eve Caplin had nothing to hide. She'd spent a small fortune creating her on paper and ten years inhabiting her as a model citizen. Unofficially, Eve Caplin had plenty of secrets. Perhaps, in time, she'd be ready to put Eve, and those secrets, behind her for good.

She stepped into the shower, steaming water washing away some of the fear. She was safer alone, in this remote corner of the world where she might be able to begin again. She'd chosen bucolic and peaceful Chelsea instead of chic Carmel or rustic Los Olivos for another reason, as well, but that was too painful to contemplate.

After wrapping herself in the comforting softness of her extra-plush bathrobe, she checked her phone for messages. The date practically popped out of the glass screen. No wonder she was feeling blue this morning, on her mother's birthday. Twenty-three years since Isabelle Walker had succumbed to ovarian cancer. In sleepy Chelsea, Eve felt closer to her memory than she had in ages.

Her melancholy faded in the face of the morning tasks that were becoming her routine. She dressed, pulled her thick black hair into a bun at the nape of her neck, and browsed through the morning's news on her laptop while sipping espresso made from her thousand-dollar machine. She'd had to drive all the way to San Luis Obispo to get it, but each life-giving sip of caffeine was worth every mile and every dollar.

Keeping up with world affairs was proving a difficult habit to break. It no longer mattered to her what was going on in Rome, or London, or Geneva, but she'd been doing it so long, on the off chance that there might be a tidbit that meant something to her, that she found she couldn't stop.

Her empty email inbox was a good sign, since John had

promised to email her if there was anything she needed to know. Leaving her partner behind when she'd departed Paris had actually been a relief. She and John would continue to stay in touch, but she no longer had to worry about him knowing her too well, so well that it could get one of them hurt, or in trouble. He'd been brilliant at identifying opportunities and helping her with the technical side of things. He'd shown her how to pick her first lock and enter and exit a secure room without leaving a trace of her presence behind. She'd been useful to him, giving him access to legitimate sellers and buyers and getting into places that even he couldn't. They'd worked out a rhythm, and it had been extremely lucrative for both of them.

They'd been a team for a decade, but it hadn't taken long for John and her to realize they would never have a romantic entanglement. They made a splendid-looking couple, he tall, blond, and athletic, she diminutive and darkly elegant, and had used their natural chemistry to their advantage more than once. But he was light and tended to the frivolous, though that hid a razor-sharp edge. He was like a beautiful and extremely sharp knife; you admired the craftsmanship, but if you handled it the wrong way, you'd get cut before you even realized it. While that was useful in a business partner, it wouldn't have suited her in a boyfriend. Not that she had much experience with what did or didn't suit her. When she'd first come to Europe, she'd rushed into several ill-advised romances with dark, exciting men, only to have her heart broken. Then when her careers—as gallery curator and art thief—both took off, she had neither the time nor the energy to properly vet prospective boyfriends, lest they be Interpol plants or too inquisitive for their own good. So the relationships, if they could be called that, had been sporadic and brief. Was loneliness another reason she'd been so ready to chuck it all and return to America, land of her unresolved issues?

Annoyed at her self-pitying introspection, Eve shut the lid of her computer with a click and inspected the kitchen with a critical eye. The appliances were all installed, and most of the furniture had been delivered. She'd been living here for less than two weeks, but so far she was ahead of schedule. Should she start thinking about repainting the walls, or get to know the area better? Los Angeles and San Francisco were both within a half day's drive if she were craving some culture. She'd always been good at finding things to occupy her time, but she'd have to get out of the house if she wanted activity. Opportunity wasn't likely to literally knock on her door out here.

A knock sounded on the front door, making her smile.

The man on the other side of the door resembled Hudson around the eyes and the chin, but his lips were thinner, and his nose a different shape altogether. His dark brown hair was straight and cut short and he wore a wide gold wedding band on his left hand.

"You must be Will," she said. "Come on in."

Will Cleary was an intelligent, efficient man who, along with his apprentice, Carlos, had her new locks installed within an hour. He presented a more than adequate plan for the rest of the security measures she'd requested, with a few more of his own ideas added in and approved by Eve.

They sat at the kitchen bar on her new stainless steel bar stools, finalizing the plans and going over the estimate.

"I met your brother the other day," Eve said, broaching a subject that had been niggling at her brain for days.

"He covers for me from time to time," Will said. "Did he do a good job?"

"Oh, yes, fine. Silly of me to lock myself out in the first place."

"It happens," Will said easily, shuffling papers back into a folder with her name on it. "I've done it myself, believe it or not."

She smiled and showed him out. Will was likable and she trusted her gut feeling that he was honest. She rested with her back to the door and thought of her lock pick set, gathering dust. If she'd had them with her the day she'd moved in, might she never have met Hudson?

She'd tried not to think about him since he'd invited her to sit for him. The idea had thrown her, and not least because she had been certain he was going to ask her out when he had that cute, nervous, talking-too-fast thing happening. But he'd asked her to model instead of to dinner and she'd actually wanted to say yes to his—request? Offer? Who would turn down a chance to work with one of the most brilliant, not to mention, gorgeous, painters of the twenty-first century?

Getting involved with a man, a painter, no less, was not part of the plan. Eve was giving herself time and the space to think, to reflect, to decide what she was going to make of her life. The last decade had been some kind of bizarre dream, where she did things that regular people—*real* people—didn't do. As a girl, she'd longed for glamour and adventure, and she'd gotten her wish, in spades. It had taken every ounce of her courage to walk away from that life and imagine a different path for herself. The still-rational part of her brain had known that if she didn't walk away, that glamorous, adventurous life would end either in jail or death. Those were two adventures she could put off indefinitely.

But a life where the most pressing matter on her plate was picking a china pattern was not as fulfilling as she'd hoped it would be. Though she'd retired from her illegal activities, she didn't want to be floating aimlessly for the rest of her life. The bulging manila envelope that sat unopened on the dining room table might have given her some direction, jump-started her progress. The name on the outside—Genevieve Walker—was the name of a stranger. She'd reinvented herself as Eve Caplin long ago and that was who she was now, for better or worse. Ruthlessly, she taped the envelope to the bottom of the table. It would be secure enough until her safe was installed. Until then, she wasn't ready to open it. She might never be ready.

Home improvements were the best form of procrastination. She put away the tape, pulled out a pile of paint chips, and started debating between Swiss Coffee and White Dove.

Chapter Four

Hudson rounded the point and slowed from a brisk jog to a fast walk. He'd tacked an extra two miles onto his regular beach run, and his thighs were burning. The sharp sea air cooled the sweat on the back of his neck and he felt invigorated, if no less frustrated.

He'd started the day the way he spent every Thursday morning, volunteering at Chelsea's single convalescent home. Tomorrow, he was giving blood; he'd stop at the diner on the way home for a burger, to fortify his iron. He'd done something unusual after returning home from reading to Mr. Rosenbaum and holding the yarn for Mrs. Sinclair's knitting project: he'd gone into his studio. Once in there, he'd sat down at his desk and started fiddling around with some images that had been rolling around in his head. They weren't only Eve's face, which he'd sketched over and over since he'd met her, each time not quite right. It had been nearly two years since he'd gone to his studio to do more than drink a beer and watch the rain fall outside the large plate glass windows that made up the entire northern wall.

Giving in to the need to sketch Eve had somehow reminded his fingers there was some life in there yet. The strangest thing remained how the large-scale abstracts he'd built his career on, that had fascinated him from his infancy as an artist, were nowhere to be found in the small pile of sketches. They were of chins, eyes, ears, recognizable features of the weathered looking man he'd seen at the gas station that morning, of his smallest niece, Caitlyn, even of Mrs. Sinclair, knitting needles and all.

He clearly had an itch, if only he knew where to scratch. If he was honest, that itch had started the day he'd set eyes on Eve Caplin, and hadn't let up.

Her rejection still stung. He couldn't console himself with the idea that he could ask her on a date. Dating had become as infrequent as studio sessions. If he could even begin to start thinking about painting again, then he could certainly manage a drink or dinner. Maybe after she got to know him, she'd reconsider. She couldn't be blamed for being wary. She was a beautiful woman, and busy, besides. Modeling wasn't everyone's thing. It could be very hard work, which if she knew art, she'd be aware of. He could tell she'd been interested; she hadn't let herself say yes.

He blew out an aggravated breath. He wanted to see her again, even more than he wanted to paint her.

He considered asking Will if he needed help completing her security system installation, since Eve had asked his brother to rush the work. But Will was close to done, plus the ruse was too hokey to work. He didn't want to see her again as an employee, anyway. He wanted to see her as a man.

He had her phone number from the day he'd let her into her house. He fished his cell phone out of the pocket of his running shorts. It would be a simple matter to press the buttons, let it ring, ask her to meet him for a drink.

He thought of her snooty little accent, her elite gallery experience, the way she'd icily dismissed his request, and he let the phone drop back into his pocket. Maybe he'd run another half a mile.

⊗

Hudson's request to paint her had been rattling around in Eve's head for days, distracting her at the oddest moments.

She'd been taken aback by the request, and her answer had been stilted; she was afraid she'd come off as horribly snobby and uptight.

She'd wanted to say yes. The thought of posing for Hudson, clothed or not, was extremely erotic. What would it feel like to submit to his eyes, to his hands, as they searched out her secrets and put them on paper? He was more than talented; he was brilliant. She'd known it the first time she'd seen one of his paintings, before she ever knew his name or the sinfully handsome face behind it.

Saying yes would have meant prolonged contact with a man who couldn't be counted on to disappear before he got too close. Men usually did what she wanted them to, eventually, but with Hudson, one couldn't know.

Even though she'd come to Chelsea to start again, to make different choices and return some semblance of normality to her existence, there were still enough messy threads from her old life tangling up with the present that it made her think twice before adding one huge complication to the mix.

And yet, she couldn't stop thinking about him.

What she needed was a new project. She'd finished appointing the interior of the house with furniture, appliances, and gadgets. The upstairs had been entirely repainted, and the security system was well in place. Her paintings had not yet arrived, so her walls were still bare. She opened the French doors and looked over her backyard, neglected brown grass that melted into a copse of native trees, over which she could see a generous band of twinkling silver ocean. Time to turn to the exterior.

With one hand, she pulled out her cell phone, scrolling down to the name of the contractor she'd met at the Home Depot in Pismo Beach. With the other, she started sketching the outlines of a deck. Nothing like endless home improvement projects to keep the mind and body off the subject of men.

After making the appointment with the contractor, Eve lost track of time, perfecting her vision for the deck. The sound of her doorbell caused her to jerk her head up. She slid the plans into a neat stack and smoothed her hair. *Always be prepared.*

The person on her doorstep was decidedly not Hudson. She was a woman of average height, slim build, but with hips and a fair amount of bosom. She wore her blond hair cropped close to her head, which made her look younger, but Eve guessed she was about thirty. She wore Levis and cowboy boots and a plain white tank top. Her arms were bronzed from sun exposure, and she had freckles on her nose. Her mouth was a generous slash and she smiled, holding up a jar of something the color of liquid amber.

"Hi, neighbor, I'm Rue. I live back down the road at Honeydale Farm, and this is some for you. Honey, that is."

Eve couldn't help the grin that split her face. "Would you like to come in for some coffee?"

Rue moved nonstop, setting the honey on the kitchen bar, inspecting the top of the line espresso machine that Eve had recently mastered. "Fancy," was her assessment, but she readily agreed to a cappuccino.

"I didn't know there was a farm nearby," Eve commented as she readied her tiny porcelain cups for the rich brew. She had a set of eight, but so far had used but one, washing it in the sink since she didn't have enough dishes to run the dishwasher. Reinventing oneself had been lonely so far. She hoped she didn't sound desperate for company, but it didn't matter. Rue continued to inspect the kitchen, chatting freely as she did so.

"It's not much of a farm, yet. I raise bees for honey and for renting to other farms, and we have some chickens, vegetables, a pig. I sell the honey at the farmers market in town, and we also sell to some fancy foodie places from Carmel to Santa Barbara."

"You're a beekeeper," Eve said in wonder.

"That's right."

"Wherever did you learn?"

"You know the usual tale. I graduated college with absolutely no direction, so I hoofed around Europe for a while. I ended up doing some woofing in England at a honeybee farm. Turns out I had a way with bees, and I stayed for a year. The owner really took me under his wing, so to speak."

Eve laughed. "Woofing?"

"WWOOFing. World Wide Opportunities on Organic Farms. You work for room and board, learn a little about farming. After I left there, I ended up at a farm in NorCal before I met my partner, Jess. That's short for Jessica, not Jesse, if you were wondering, and she found this place selling in a short sale, so we scraped together the down payment. She's a vet tech."

Eve was startled when the flow of words stopped.

Rue was taking a sip of the cappuccino and moaning. "Damn, that's good. I haven't had espresso that fine since Paris."

"Thanks."

"So, what's your story?"

Eve was both unsettled and refreshed by the directness of the question. "I'm new to the area."

"No kidding. You look like a French model and you talk like you've watched one too many episodes of *Downton Abbey*."

"Um, thanks?" Did everyone think she was that exotic, and was that a bad thing? "Well, I did spend a number of years in Europe. I helped run art galleries in London, Paris, and Vienna. But I grew up in San Francisco."

"So you decided to move to backwoods Central California?"

"It's not turning out to be as backwoods as I imagined," she said, thinking of Hudson.

"I blame Coppola. One movie director thinking he's a winemaker and now you've got scads of Hollywood types buying up wineries right and left. The ones that can't afford Sonoma buy here."

Eve laughed again. She couldn't remember the last time she'd felt so light. "You've got more than the Hollywood types. Did you know you have a world-famous artist living right here in Chelsea? Hudson Cleary."

"Sure, I know Hudson," Rue said. "We both volunteer at the community garden behind City Hall. Nice guy."

Eve couldn't decide if she was more surprised by the way the two knew one another, or the characterization of Hudson as a nice guy. Nice was an entirely inadequate word.

"How do you know him? I know there's a story there; I have a sixth sense for gossip," Rue asked.

Eve wanted to share. It had been so long since she'd talked to a woman without having a hidden agenda. She described being locked out of her house on her first day in town, and Hudson being her locksmith's brother.

"Imagine my surprise to find out that the man unlocking my front door painted an abstract I sold for seven figures last year."

"Seven figures?" Rue whistled. "For that kind of money, I wonder why he stopped painting."

"What do you mean?"

"Everyone in town knows he has that big Craftsman house on the edge of town, with a gorgeous studio that he built, but he never works in it. His cleaning lady told me it's practically empty. It's been that way for a couple of years," Rue said, helping herself to one of the biscotti Eve had set out along with the cappuccinos.

"That can't be right. Maybe he works someplace else." She couldn't imagine someone as talented and successful as Hudson giving it all up to go work in a community garden, and he'd also asked her to sit for him. "He even asked me...." Was it too personal to share?

"Asked you what? Spill."

"He asked me to sit for him. The other day when he came back to take some measurements for his brother."

"You mean, like, model?" Rue laughed. "What a great line. Not that you couldn't be a model. Jess is going to hate you when she meets you," she said cheerfully. "But as far as I know, he's retired. I've never seen him with paint on his hands or anything."

"Huh." Eve needed some time to process that information. "So what does he do? He told me he fills in as a locksmith from time to time."

"He doesn't have a regular job, as far as I know, but he

volunteers pretty much anywhere that'll take him in town. The garden is one of his projects."

"Really? That's...perplexing."

Rue shrugged. "Maybe he likes giving back. He's not sanctimonious about it or anything. I've had him over a few times for Sunday Supper, but he usually doesn't talk much about himself. He'll talk your ear off about these old people he's friends with down at the convalescent home, though."

Eve was getting more confused by the second. "Talk your ear off?"

"Well, in relative terms. He's not exactly a chatty guy."

"No. Well, I guess we all have unexpected sides."

"And he doesn't have a bad one." At Eve's stare, Rue grinned. "What? I'm not blind. He's a very attractive male specimen, if you like that sort of thing."

"That's an understatement."

"Sounds like you've already made up your mind. You wouldn't mind 'sitting' for him at all." Innuendo laced her words.

"No! Well, the thought had crossed my mind, to be honest. I thought he was genuine. He's a brilliant artist."

"I'm imagining you'd show up to his studio and he'd be there, Burt Reynolds-style, buck naked on a bear skin rug."

"Please, give me a little more credit than that."

"I'm sure you've had your share of bad come-ons before. Beautiful American in a classy gallery?"

"No, well, maybe. It's been a while since I've wanted to take someone up on it."

"Well, as I said, he's a nice guy, as far as I know. But everyone has secrets."

"Don't I know it," Eve said.

"I've got to get back to work. Thanks for the caffeine and the sugar."

Eve showed her to the door. "Thanks for being neighborly. And for the honey."

"You should stop by for our Sunday Supper. Nice people, fresh food, lots of wine."

"I'd love to."

She waved as Rue walked back down the hill. Getting close to her neighbors could be a mistake. It felt wonderful, being accepted into a community, but it made her cautious. So many things could go so very wrong.

Chapter Five

*H*udson woke with a headache that the bright white California sunlight had only worsened. He never over-indulged in alcohol, so he wasn't hung over, and he didn't suffer from allergies. He blamed the ache in his skull on his poor night of sleep, caused by an over-preoccupation with the brunette who lived at the top of Oak Grove Hill.

He'd resisted her pull all week, the way he might resist stopping in at the doughnut shop when he was trying to curb his coffee and maple bar habit for a while. Just as he was always drawn back into the caffeine and sugar thrall, so would he turn up on Eve Caplin's doorstep.

He took two pain relievers and stomped around the house for a while. He thought about going to the studio, but the half-finished sketches on his worktable mocked him even from afar. He hadn't been able to recapture the first burst of creative energy, and wished he'd never had it in the first place.

He was desperate to relieve some of this pressure, and if the only way was by making a fool of himself with Eve yet again, then so be it.

The drive to her house was disconcertingly short. He barely had time to rehearse what he was going to say. All he could think about was how much she intrigued him, and how much he either needed her in his bed or in his studio so he could unlock some of the tension that had been building since he met her.

She was home. He drove onto the driveway, knowing she'd hear his tires on the gravel, giving himself no out.

A contractor's truck was parked to the side of the house, and a couple of men with tool belts around their hips walked from the vehicle to the rear of the house, carrying lumber and bags of cement.

Hudson revised his approach. Trying to abide by the usual channels with Eve would result in one blocked move after another. Instead, he went around the back, to find a small crew blocking out what appeared to be a generously sized deck. The wind had picked up here on the top of the hill, and Eve's long hair whipped around her face as she consulted with a small mountain of a man who was probably the foreman. She was talking and he was nodding. No doubt she was detailing exactly what she wanted, in no uncertain terms.

When she saw him standing on the edge of the yard, her eyebrows jerked up, but there was a flicker of a smile before her mouth turned neutral. Enough to give him hope. He waited until she was done speaking with the foreman, then sauntered up, offering her a casual grin, letting her draw her own conclusions about his presence there.

"Hello," she said. "What can I do for you?"

He wanted to answer with something more provocative, but first things first. "A cup of coffee would do, for now."

"All right," she said, and led the way through the French doors.

"You're building a deck," he observed. "Good for property value."

"And for looking at my view," she said as she started the espresso machine. "Americano?"

"Why don't you give me a straight shot?"

Her movements were economical as she went about tamping freshly ground beans into the filter. He was impressed that she had a full-fledged espresso machine, not a pre-done cup one.

"Have you thought about putting up a fence at your property line? A woman as security conscious as you must hate anyone being able to walk around your entire house."

"J.J. is already working some numbers up for me. I'll have to see how his crew does with the deck, but so far they seem dependable."

"You're one step ahead of me."

Eve smiled but let the comment slide. "I met one of my neighbors the other day. A beekeeper named Rue. She says she knows you."

"That's right. She and her girlfriend own that piece of land down the hill from you." He eyed the jar of honey on the counter. "Their honey is pricey, but delicious."

"Would you like a taste?"

He moved his gaze from the honey to her lips. "Sure."

She turned away quickly, busying herself pouring out his espresso and then rummaging in a drawer for a spoon that she then dipped in the jar. A golden thread of honey streamed from the spoon to the glass container. Eve broke it with a finger that she brought to her mouth.

He was already hard when he took the spoonful of honey she offered him and licked the sticky sweetness. It tasted like sunshine and sage blossoms and he wanted to spread it over Eve's lips and nibble away the afternoon.

"Sweet," he murmured.

"Isn't it? Rue was very kind to stop by. I didn't know neighbors still did that," she said, a girlish smile on her face. She seemed young and happy, like a Degas pastel come to life.

"It must be hard to move to a new place without knowing anyone."

"Yes," she said. "Though now I know Rue. And you, I suppose." She said the last part grudgingly.

"I'd like to know you better," he said, venturing into the subject that stood like a brick wall between them.

She stared at him, tucked her hair behind her ears.

"If you start with that cold-as-ice thanks-for-your-interest bull, I won't be responsible for my actions," he said reasonably. He took a sip of espresso. The bitter chased away the sweet. He wanted that sweet back.

She sighed. Her shoulders dropped and her mouth softened. "I'd like to know you better, too."

That was all the invitation he needed. He rose off the bar stool and was at her side in two strides. He waited, smelling the brewed coffee mingled with her scent, fresh and subtle, and then when he couldn't stand it anymore, he slid one hand up the back of her neck and cupped the nape, the gentle pressure of his fingers pushing her lips closer to his.

Eve was transfixed.

She couldn't look anywhere but at those gorgeously molded lips. The fact that they parted for her made her feel like someone had flipped a switch that sent hot, pulsing currents of electricity through her belly, her legs, her breasts. Her heart beat fast and hard, and when lips met lips, it might have stopped and stumbled for a moment before resuming its clattering against her ribs. He was soft, the kiss light, as if he were afraid to deepen it. Eve was aware of nothing but the spark that was going to light a bonfire between them as surely as she breathed. It didn't matter if the kiss was as chaste as a schoolgirl kissing the back of her own hand. They were headed someplace hot and heavy, and they both knew it.

She was drowning in the overwhelming pleasure of being near him. She couldn't think, couldn't see, couldn't breathe. There was only him. His arms held her close while his hands, those clever painter's hands, touched and probed, teased her skin, her hair, wriggled their way under her clothes to touch places on her body that no one but she had touched in a very long time.

The sensations came at her both too fast and not fast enough. She leaned into the embrace, kissing him back as though he alone carried the oxygen she needed to survive. She was terrified as she threw herself against him, more afraid to look back, to stop, to live life without this exquisite intensity.

A noise came from some distant place. Hudson moved slightly away, and Eve recognized the sound of someone pointedly clearing his throat.

"Wow," she breathed, before coming fully back into the present.

J.J., the foreman, stood in the doorway. "We're going to start pouring the foundation now, Ms. Caplin. You asked me to let you know."

"Oh, right. Thanks."

When they were alone again, she allowed herself to look at Hudson's face. He was smiling, satisfied as if she'd given him the right answer to a question.

"Well," she said a little more briskly. "That was nice."

"Mmm. Very nice," he agreed, his eyes crinkling.

Eve was suddenly annoyed by how very handsome he was, by his calm. She stepped back. "Your espresso's getting cold."

"So are you."

She lifted her chin and regarded him, her spine stiffening. "Now that you've gotten what you came for, maybe you should leave."

"All right," he said easily.

He was infuriating.

He rose and went to door they'd entered from. "But I haven't had nearly enough."

Huffing, she turned away, refusing to watch him leave. She poured the rest of his coffee down the drain with relish. She'd been knocked for a loop, as they say, by one kiss, and she didn't like it one bit. Hudson had made her see stars, then smiled like he'd crossed some item off his to-do list.

And she'd forgotten to ask him about his work. She was interested from a purely professional standpoint, of course, that one of the most successful painters of the day was not painting. And if he wasn't, she wanted to know why he'd asked her to sit for him in the first place. It hadn't felt like a line, but now that he'd managed to get his hands on her without any of that folderol, she couldn't trust her instincts. She pushed the thought away, and went outside to watch concrete pouring into some holes.

Chapter Six

*B*y midday Tuesday, the deck construction was going so well that Eve planned to be sitting on it, sipping her coffee and watching the morning clouds burn off over the Pacific, by the weekend. The symphony of hammers, saws, and the rapid Spanish-language deejay chatter emanating from the contractor's truck stereo was a comfort and a welcome distraction. She couldn't unpack the crate of paintings that had arrived at the end of the day yesterday with the workers in the back, so she'd given up trying to get anything else accomplished and sat at the kitchen bar doing last Sunday's crossword puzzle. The doorbell rang in a lull of construction noise, startling her.

Expecting the FedEx man bearing her new food processor, she flung the door open. A tall, lanky blond with faded blue eyes and an entirely too smug grin stood on her doorstep. He carried a leather weekender bag and nothing else. The only car in the drive was her three-day-old silver sedan.

Eve swore, briefly and colorfully, as John Norton dropped his bag and lifted her up in his arms in a bear hug. She let out a squeak as he plopped her back on the front step, chortling at her astonishment.

"I surprised you, didn't I, Evie?" He preened a little, adjusting the collar of his designer polo shirt.

"That's an understatement." She wasn't ready to be gracious

to her old partner quite yet. "Well, you better come in." Resigned to the not entirely unwelcome intrusion, she followed him into the house.

"Give me the five cent tour, Evie darling," he said. "Which room is mine?"

John hadn't changed in the long weeks since she'd last seen him. He was still entitled, fussy, and vain, but in such an endearing way that she sighed and led him to the newly painted guest room. She accepted his compliments on her home with short patience.

"What I want to know is how you found me. And don't give me some line about IP addresses."

"Maurice," John said simply.

Eve swore for the second time that day.

"But I didn't tell him...oh, the paintings."

"The paintings," John agreed.

Eve had given everything up when she'd left Paris. Her flat, her job, even a safe deposit box full of odds and ends in Geneva that she hadn't had time to go back for, but she couldn't leave behind her paintings. They were how she'd invested her earnings, sometimes using laundered money to purchase perfectly legitimate items at auction or estate sales, sometimes taking less than pristine goods in trade for her merchandise. Those paintings were her savings and retirement plan all rolled into one, but they were also a reflection of her taste. She didn't buy anything she didn't like. Who knew when she would be able to sell some of the pieces, so she decided she'd better be able to live with them in the meantime.

Maurice, an old contact and one she trusted, had promised her he could get them into the country—"get" being a euphemism for "smuggle"—and she'd paid him a small fortune to do so. She'd given him the address of an import house in San Francisco, and then had the goods forwarded to her from there. He could have tracked down the final destination if he'd needed to, but she didn't really think he'd have to bother. John apparently had.

"Congratulations, Sherlock, you tracked me down. Now, what's it all about?"

"As much as I missed your funny little face, Evie darling, this is not a purely social call."

The knots in her stomach tightened. "It's him, isn't it?"

"Deacon? Yes." John paused. "He wants something from you."

Her stomach clenched, and the knots turned into a lead weight. How could this be happening so soon?

"Dammit." Her voice shook a little. "I don't owe that man anything. I know he thinks we queered the Chagall job for him, but the man is a lunatic. We didn't know he was planning to go for it." She stopped her rant. John had heard this all before, but venting helped the fear morph into anger. "Wait. How do you know he wants something from me? Was he specific, or does he just want my blood?"

"Let's talk about it over lunch. Your treat."

☙

"How quaint," John remarked as the blue-haired waitress at Maude's Diner shuffled away with their orders. Eve had picked the greasiest spoon in Chelsea to needle her ex-partner, who had once brought an entire five-course dinner from The Ritz on a stakeout.

"I met with him," he said. "Well, he maneuvered me into a meeting. I thought for your sake I had better take it."

"You met him," she repeated. "That could have been incredibly dangerous. It could have been a set up. He could have called the authorities. What were you thinking?"

"Darling, I do believe you care," he said sardonically.

"John." His name was a warning. She was losing patience.

"Don't worry so much. I had a backup plan."

"I know all about your backup plans," she grumbled. "So what did he say?"

"He claims that you owe him for the Chagall, as losing the

commission on it cost him with some unsavory Turks. He also knows you're in America. He proposes you do a job for him here, and you're Even Steven."

"How does he know I'm in America?" She was calculating how quickly she could be on a plane to Indonesia, Peru, maybe Jamaica. Her California interlude had been much too brief. Perhaps her plan to start over had been naïve. On the other hand, the momentary peace she'd found in Chelsea might be worth fighting for.

"That man knows everything. He's very well connected. It's not so hard to figure out. You are an American, after all."

"He doesn't know exactly where I am, though, does he?" Eve looked around her as though Deacon could see her this very moment.

"I don't think so, but the job he wants you to do is in Montecito, so it's possible that he knows you are somewhere on the west coast. Not that he'd hesitate to drag you from Maine in order to get what he wants. He's desperate."

Eve focused on the details to keep the roiling in her stomach at bay. "Montecito?" She pulled up a map on her phone. The small, moneyed community was about one hundred and forty miles south, near Santa Barbara. Eve had never been there, but the proximity to her current location chilled her. Deacon was not someone you wanted keeping tabs on you. She had moved six thousand miles to ensure that wouldn't happen.

"I don't like this, John." She wasn't ready to admit to him she was scared, so she held onto her outraged bravado a little longer. "I have no intention of doing a job, any job, for him or anyone else. I'm retired. He can go to hell."

John waited while she got it out of her system. He signaled to the waitress for the check, and calmly placed a few bills on the tray after she brought it. He continued to say nothing as Eve drained her iced tea in an uncharacteristically noisy fashion.

His silence made the severity of the situation really sink in. She'd be a fool if she didn't at least find out what Deacon wanted her to do. Her newfound sense of peace would never be recovered if she feared revenge from a ruthless criminal around every corner.

When they were in the privacy of the car again, she sighed. "What's the job?"

☙

Hudson parked his truck in a spot half a block down from the diner. He'd had a difficult morning; Mrs. Sinclair had had a small stroke and he'd spent the morning reading to her, even though she seemed to be asleep most of the time. He was starving and sad. He'd had Stephanie on the brain ever since. His sister had died in a hospital bed much like Mrs. Sinclair's, their mother reading to her from her favorite book, or so he'd been told, since he'd been on the other side of the country when his little sister had passed away.

The promise of a burger and a cherry cola was the only thing getting him through the hour.

He spotted Eve right away, that luscious cape of raven black hair contrasting with a billowy white blouse that hid all her good parts. She'd stepped out of the diner with a look of concentration and irritation. She wasn't alone. A tall blond man whose crisp polo and khakis screamed "tourist" was getting into the passenger seat of her new car. Hudson didn't care for the tightening in his chest and the way his hands were suddenly clamped hard around his poor, defenseless steering wheel.

Eve cultivated mystery about herself as easily as dandelions cropped up in the community garden's vegetable patch. He knew next to nothing about her, but she wouldn't have kissed him if she'd been involved with someone else. Even so, that slick guy didn't look like her brother.

He forced himself out of the truck and into the diner. Food would improve his outlook on the world. Another stolen kiss would, too. He'd had to consciously stop himself from driving over to Oak Grove Hill to get another taste of those honey-sweet lips every hour since he'd left her standing in that kitchen all mussed and frosty. She could put on the ice queen routine, but he knew firsthand that her mouth was hot and eager. After he ate and helped his sister-in-law set up the summer school bake sale, a friendly visit up to Eve's to see how the deck was coming along was in order.

○○

Eve poured herself a glass of Chardonnay and contemplated the setting sun through the French doors that led to her half-finished deck. She imagined future evenings like this, settling into a deck chair, watching the Pacific turn into an ocean of gold, then pink, then inky black. Perhaps Hudson would be with her, holding her to him, pressing those wicked kisses to her jaw, distracting her from the beauty of the sunset by lighting a flame of desire inside her.

She squeezed her thighs together. Apparently, she didn't even need the man in the flesh to experience a stab of desire so fierce, she wanted to cry with frustration. She sipped the wine and turned back to where John was rummaging in her fridge for the makings of dinner.

Though John had been the bearer of bad news, she was glad to have the company. Exiling oneself tended to be lonely.

The doorbell rang, and he volunteered to answer it.

"This time, it must be FedEx with my food processor."

Alone again, Hudson dogged her thoughts. She hadn't seen him since he'd kissed her. She'd been wondering when she'd next see him, if he'd ask her to pose for him again. No, with the complication of Deacon's demands, better if she kept her distance. She couldn't help reliving the moment when he'd drawn her to him and put his lips on hers. She would never forget his spicy male scent or his arms like steel as they held her while she delighted in his embrace. She put a finger to her mouth, as if to prove to herself it had happened.

She heard male voices. John was talking with someone, and then the voices grew louder. Hudson followed John into the kitchen. Damn him, he was even handsomer than she remembered. He wore an untucked flannel shirt over a plain white T-shirt and jeans. His healthy five o'clock shadow made him look a bit disreputable, but it framed the lips she'd just been thinking about. The knowledge of how they felt made her somehow vulnerable. He knew something about her that no one else on earth did, that they'd kissed. A blush warmed her cheeks.

What was worse was that John took it all in with a glance—Hudson's half smile, her blush—and was surely drawing his own conclusions.

"Hello," she said, once she realized no one was speaking.

"Hello," Hudson said.

What was he doing here?

John fluidly took over the role of host. "Won't you have some wine?" he asked, pulling out a glass for a fresh pour.

"That would be nice, thanks," Hudson said.

His focus hadn't left Eve's face. Why was that enough to make her forget herself? She forced herself to return to a neutral tone.

"John, this is Hudson Cleary, he's the brother of my security man." She paused for a sip of wine. "Hudson, this is John Norton, an old friend of mine."

"We met at the door," Hudson said.

"Hudson Cleary, the painter?" John said.

"That's right," Eve said.

"Remarkable," John murmured.

"What brings you by?" She hoped to sound nonchalant, as if she hadn't just been imagining him seducing her on her future deck.

Hudson seemed to struggle with what to say. John glanced between the two of them, and stepped forward. "We were going to put together a quick dinner. Won't you join us?"

Eve felt oddly self-conscious over John's use of "we" and "us." It made them sound like a couple. She didn't want Hudson to assume she was with John, even if it might have been safer for him to think she was off limits.

John didn't wait for Hudson's reply; he began gathering the ingredients for pesto from the refrigerator.

"All right," Hudson said. "Thanks. I wanted to see the progress on the house."

John obviously had dinner well in hand. She was a decent cook, but he had a magic touch, and she'd seen the way he'd salivated over her marble-topped island and beautiful cookware. "I'll show you the deck. It should be finished in a couple of days."

She opened the French door and stepped out into the dark. The motion sensor light flooded the workspace in a bright yellow glow. The bones of the deck, its reclaimed wood settled into a sturdy foundation, were complete. The far side had about six feet already laid. She balanced carefully on one of the supporting beams, though the drop to the gravel below was only a foot.

"This is going to be spectacular," Hudson said.

He wasn't looking anywhere but her. The realization that he hadn't abandoned his pursuit of her made Eve lose her balance. He reached out, steadying her with a touch to her elbow. His hand was warm, strong.

She shivered. Conflict roiled in her chest. How could he be the cause of her losing her footing at the same time he was by her side, there to steady her again? He consistently set off alarm bells in her brain. If they shared mere physical attraction, she could have persuaded herself that no harm would come from indulging herself. He'd understand the limits of their relationship, and she could feel free to have fun. But Hudson looked at her with a possessiveness that made a casual fling impossible. Without either of them saying the words, he would want more than she would be able to give. John's coming here, bringing an unwelcome piece of her past with him, made everything that much more off-limits. She couldn't afford to let herself have what she wanted. It wouldn't be safe for Hudson, and that meant it wouldn't be safe for her. She couldn't have an innocent bystander ruin her concentration when the stakes were life and death. This was why she'd barely dated in the last years. No, she had to be strong and keep him at arm's length from now on.

Hudson felt her pull away from him, and he wanted to bare his teeth out of the familiar pang of frustration. Why was she so determined to deny what was going on between them? He ordered himself to take a deep breath. He wasn't one for hurrying things up, whether it was a woman or a painting. He let the energy flow, let creations unfold at their own pace. With Eve, he wanted to rush, to say "to Hell" with whatever she wanted and throw her over his shoulder, march her up those stairs to that feminine, frilly bedroom of hers, and sink himself into her, possessing her, owning her. He'd never felt such sheer animal desire for a woman before.

That approach would likely land him even farther away from her than before, so he leaned back, giving her space to come in off the deck beam by herself. It seemed to work, because as long as he kept a fair amount of space between them, she relaxed, and continued to show him the improvements on the house. When they got to the hallway, she bit her lip and he tracked her gaze to a large packing crate. One side of the wooden box had been pried off. Its contents were hidden, but then he noticed a tender little portrait in the Rembrandt school leaning against the wall, its obviously old wooden frame resting on the floor. He bent forward to take a closer look. Even as a Rembrandt school original, the painting was in exceptional shape and of beautiful quality, but as he continued to study it, he knew, the way dowsers can find water by smell and a second sight, that he wasn't looking at an imitation.

An actual Rembrandt. His first thought was that he wanted to see it in better light, to look at the colors, to see how time had altered the pigments. The second was, it must have been worth a small fortune. How was a former assistant curator in possession of a Rembrandt original?

The prickle on his skin no longer had to do with the nearness of the delectable Eve, but with the fact that there could easily be a dozen more paintings inside that crate, and something told him they were each going to be as astonishing, and as valuable, as that precious Rembrandt.

She'd meant to take him up to the second floor to see the fresh paint in the guest room, but they had to walk by the crate to get there. She was ready to tell him they were the light fixtures she'd ordered for the deck, but never got the chance.

Eve choked on her own stupidity as soon as she saw the Rembrandt propped against the wall where she'd left it. Why hadn't she packed it away the moment she'd assured herself that the paintings had arrived in one piece? From the way Hudson was staring at it, then at her, she would not be able to sell him the "very good reproduction" line. He was a painter, and a genius one, to boot. He could tell fellow genius when he saw it. Damn.

Her brain kicked into overdrive to think of a way to deflect the situation, to con Hudson into believing the portrait of a man in a feathered hat was indeed a copy, when she became aware of an unsettling truth.

She didn't want to.

A part of her wanted to tell Hudson exactly why a Rembrandt lay in the middle of her hallway, and why a dangerous thief named Deacon expected her to steal a priceless painting in a scant week. She could own up to why she'd come to this middle of nowhere town. She could confess that her air of sophistication and respectability masked an undeniable criminal past.

She craved telling him all of that, and more. How the way he looked at her made her feel treasured and his touch made her long for more. How she'd gladly bare her body for him to paint if only he'd use those clever hands on her once he was finished.

Her intuition, normally her greatest asset when negotiating a tricky job, was telling her that if she did tell him the truth, maybe not all of it, but some, he would listen and perhaps understand.

Eve was thus caught between hope and fear. How could she expect a creator of great art to understand someone who stole it?

She held his gaze for a long moment, waited for questions,

demands.

Hudson reached out.

She didn't understand what he was doing until he was holding her hand as if it were as fragile as a Limoges figurine.

"Are you in some kind of trouble?" he asked, his voice unexpectedly gentle.

For some reason, her eyes grew wet and she took a gulp of air. His gesture threw her off balance even more than her attraction to him.

"I—"

A crash from the kitchen made them both turn their heads. John let out a long, mostly unintelligible curse, then called cheerily, "Everything's okay!"

She couldn't help a small smile as she let out a long breath. Hudson relaxed his posture, but held onto her hand.

"Hudson—"

"You know what, Eve? I don't want to be lied to. You don't have to tell me if you don't want to, but please, don't lie to me."

She nodded. Her silence was his answer.

"Do I want to see what else is in that crate?"

If she was going to hang some of its contents anyway, Hudson would see them. He'd be back. Hard to keep someone at a distance when you wanted them right by your side.

"I suppose you're more interested in these than in the color I painted the guest room."

"You can show me that later."

She knelt down next to the crate, pulling him down with her instead of releasing his hand.

"I packed these a while ago," she said, taking out the next carefully wrapped item. "I'm not sure exactly...oh, of course!"

She uncovered an oil of a stark gray farmhouse sitting in the middle of a field. "This will look perfect in the library!" Her unease had been replaced with delight at meeting her old friends again.

"Is that a Wyeth?" Hudson asked.

"Yes. Andrew."

"Gorgeous," he said. "His use of color matches the drama of the Maine landscape to perfection."

He helped her pull out a larger piece. Together, they unwrapped it to find a mostly white canvas, with gray lines running in geometric patterns.

"Richard Tuttle?" he guessed.

"Agnes Martin."

"You have exquisite, if eclectic, taste."

Hudson seemed as excited as she to see what treasure would next emerge from the shipping container. His comments stoked her own enthusiasm and she eagerly brought out another to show him. Each painting revealed another aspect of her soul, whether he realized it or not, and bound them together tighter than all of the secrets left unsaid.

Hudson stared at the charming oil still life of flowers and fruit as Eve finished unwrapping it. "I can see why you wanted all that security."

She shoved a pile of bubble wrap and newspaper back in the crate and held the painting away from her. "Yes."

"That's from his later work," Hudson said, much more casually than he felt. The artist was Paul Cézanne, the painting worth millions.

"It's my favorite," she said quietly.

As she placed it carefully next to the others, he rose, surveying the fortune in artwork that was lined up against the wall, wondering about their owner. This house was beautiful, modern, but not flashy or in a particularly expensive location. She had to be loaded to own a collection like this. He'd never speculated about her arrival in Chelsea, her casual spending of thousands to furnish her home in record time, to outfit it with the best security money could buy. His brother had been smiling for weeks with the boost having her as a client had brought his small company. Will had been talking about moving further into the high-end market, servicing the reclusive wealthy who lived scattered around the coast.

Maybe she was a dot com investor, or inherited a wad of dough from an elderly millionaire she'd married for the money. Maybe she was a bank robber. Did it matter?

Her silence when he'd told her not to lie to him led him to believe she'd acquired these pieces in a less than up and up way. That her past was unknown to him both excited him and made him worried for her. Why should he be afraid for a woman he barely knew? She brought out a protective side in him that he'd thought reserved for his nieces and sister.

Though there wasn't anything else that was brotherly about the way he felt about her.

John rang the proverbial dinner gong and ushered them to the table. Hudson was glad for the distraction both from Eve and the mesmerizing pull of those priceless paintings.

Dinner was surprisingly delicious, with the two bottles of crisp Chardonnay accompanying the meal helping conversation flow easily between the three of them.

Though he'd been initially reserved, and, if he was honest with himself, a little jealous, he warmed up to John. The man was witty and kept the tone of the evening light.

Hudson was surprised when he asked questions bordering on the personal that Eve and John answered as if they had nothing to hide. Perhaps he was imagining things, and they were simply two old friends, one passing through town, the other starting over in a fresh place.

"So, how did you two meet?" John asked, between bites of pesto linguine.

Eve glanced at Hudson, an amused look in her eyes. "You'll never believe this, but I locked myself out the very first day I got here. Hudson came to let me in."

"A man of many talents," John said.

"Rather."

Hudson cleared his throat as a blush swept over Eve's cheeks, reminding him of every wicked thing he wanted to do to her. "My brother's a locksmith, I was covering for him," he said. "So how far back do you two go?"

"Oh, donkey's years," John said.

"I don't want to think about how long, it will make me feel old," Eve said.

"School chums?" Hudson asked.

"No. I met John though his father. He introduced us and we hit it off as friends, did some traveling together."

"Oh? Whereabouts?"

"Mostly southern Europe. There was one trip to Moscow," John said.

"And Morocco."

"Oh, yes, Casablanca. Believe me, it's not as romantic as it sounds."

"As I recall, you were dating that stuck up girl and she thought the perfectly nice hotel we were staying at was as bad as a backpacker's hostel."

"She left after one night, accusing me of forcing her to rough it," John said, rolling his eyes. "We were at a three star hotel!"

Hudson and Eve laughed. "Sounds like fun," he said. "I've never been to North Africa. I spent about a year traveling around Europe with a buddy of mine after my first big show. The sophomore slump loomed large in my mind, so I decided to get away for a while."

John seemed eager to latch on to the topic of Hudson's career. "Tell us more about yourself, Hudson. It's not every day that one shares dinner with a world famous painter."

Outside of his family and a handful of suppers at Rue's place down the hill, he wasn't accustomed to sharing dinner with anyone. In the past couple of years, he'd taken the reclusive artist bit to heart. Easier to pretend he was an eccentric than admit to grief, guilt, and being a has-been. It felt good to be among friends—well, he could stretch and call them that—eating something more interesting than diner food.

"I grew up in Chelsea, escaped as quickly as I could to San Francisco, spent some time in New York, and came back a couple of years ago when my sister passed away and my parents moved to Paso Robles."

"I'm sorry," Eve said softly. "She must have been young."

Hudson hesitated. He'd surprised himself by mentioning Stephanie at all. Eve's face showed sincere sympathy that made him wish he were alone with her. Maybe he could tell her the entire story. Maybe she'd understand. Or maybe she'd regret ever trying to get to know him better.

"She was thirty. She had a fast moving type of cancer. I had always planned to move back to Chelsea, and my brother and his wife live here with their three kids. I like to play the doting uncle."

"You find you like the peace and quiet?" John asked, as if the concept left a bad taste in his mouth.

Hudson laughed. "I do."

"You should try it sometime, John. It's very refreshing," Eve said.

"I give it six months, tops. Our Evie's a city girl at heart."

"I'm trying something new," she said tightly. "And I like it. Really."

The men burst out laughing at her protestations.

John hung back in the kitchen when Hudson made his move to go.

"A pleasure, Hudson," he said formally. "I'm sure we'll meet again." Then he winked at Eve, making her roll her eyes.

Hudson laughed, and allowed Eve to lead him out of the room toward the front door. She stepped out with him onto the narrow front porch, shutting the door behind her. The night was black as pitch, but so clear they could see stars like so much confetti at Times Square on New Year's. The salt-flavored air was chilly, and she rubbed her bare arms.

He reached out, to warm her, perhaps to give in to the desire he'd had all night to hold her, but she stepped back.

"I don't think it's a good idea for us to get closer," she said.

He had been looking at her face, smelling her, hearing her laugh all night, and he was at the end of his short leash of self-control. On some primitive level of his cognition, she was right. Touching her wasn't a good idea at all. It would lead them both down a path they would rather not be on.

The war raging in him caused his frustration, his impatience, his sheer lust to rise to the surface, and he almost growled as he disregarded her words and crushed her to him, covering her mouth with his, increasing his grip with blatant satisfaction when she instantly melted into him, opening her mouth readily to his, belying all her careful protestations.

They fused together, time and place and words all falling away, blood and heat and unadulterated passion rising up. His hands were in that gorgeous mass of hair, his mouth wanted to be everywhere. She pressed herself to him as desperately, filling his male need to be wanted, to be needed.

If there hadn't been a curious Englishman inside the house, Hudson would have pulled her back in, dragged her up those stairs, and taken everything he wanted. They might not even make it up the stairs. He'd have her anywhere, take her everywhere. As he pictured her delicate body naked under his, she stepped away. He couldn't fulfill this promise to himself until she wanted it as much as he.

He released her slowly, holding them both steady as they caught their breaths. He could wait. "Thanks for dinner," he said in a low voice, then let her go, disappearing into the inky black. She didn't wait for him to drive away, but retreated back into the house. His heart raced so loudly he could hear his own pulse over the roar of his pickup as he backed it up and turned it toward town.

Chapter Seven

*E*ve was going to have to make do with the memory of two soul-altering kisses. She'd never had a use for passion. Passion made you sloppy and got you caught. She was always cerebral when it came to her life—so cerebral that men were only pawns to get what she needed. Those kisses had kept her awake half the night, her mind unable to stop replaying every searing detail. She assembled the ingredients for French toast, sugar being her regular antidote to the lethargy of a bad night's sleep.

She had never met a man who made her want to be a different person, a better person. For the first time, she felt ashamed of her past. How would Hudson react if she told him she'd broken laws in six countries, stolen millions of dollars worth of paintings from mostly innocent people? Would he be impressed that she could pick any lock in under thirty seconds, or run for the hills?

He didn't seem so sanctimonious that he might turn her in, but she didn't think he would be happy, either. She wasn't entirely happy with herself. There was passion between them, yes, but there was also a deeper link, and that connection couldn't be made real and whole unless they were honest with one another. She couldn't have a relationship with him if she was hiding a ten-year chapter of her life from him every minute of every day. If he'd been a man without demands, whom she could be merely comfortable with, perhaps she could leave her old life behind as she'd planned and feel okay about not revealing that side of herself. She could get a regular job, get married, have babies, and no one would have to know.

But he was Hudson. He would have to know. She longed to have the freedom to open herself up to him all the way. She pictured his reaction if she told him the truth. He'd recoil, shocked, angry, or she didn't know him very well. Eve laughed at the sentiment. She didn't know him at all, and she was contemplating his reaction to her deepest secrets. The chance of them getting to that point was nil.

He wasn't coming any closer to her. She couldn't let him.

All that was left of the French toast when John entered the kitchen was a plate sticky with syrup. For the first time, Eve noticed how thin he was, how his eyes were ringed by purple smudges.

"Are you all right?" she asked sympathetically as she poured him some strong coffee.

"Jet lag," he said, downing half a cup. His hands were a bit shaky when she topped him up.

"How long are you staying?" she asked as she put together a simple chopped salad for lunch. The men working on the deck were on their own lunch break in the shade of the trees behind her house.

"I have to leave tomorrow, but I'll meet you in Montecito for the gig next week. If you decide to do it, that is."

She set the salad bowl down hard on the bar. "You know I have to do it, John, but it galls me."

"Let's get it over with and then Deacon will leave us alone."

She wanted to believe that. She tried to get herself into the brisk, businesslike mindset that helped her quell her nerves before she plunged into a dangerous job. "Tell me the details. I was so annoyed yesterday I didn't listen very closely."

"It's a Mondrian. About a foot and a half square. Worth ten

mil. Some rich businessman is giving it on permanent loan to the Santa Barbara Art Museum. It will be on display for one night only, that's next Friday night, a week from tomorrow, at the bloke's house in Montecito. There's a fundraiser that night. Should be a couple of hundred people. We can get in, scope out the security, then come back later and lift the painting. Delivery is by Saturday at noon."

Eve imagined the chain of events. They'd handled worse situations on shorter notice. "It sounds straightforward enough. Can we find a hole in the security with that little prep time?"

"We'll have to. It has to be that night. Apparently, the painting is stored in a vault until then, and the next day, it will be transported to the museum. We don't have time to pull off an in-transit switch or anything like that."

John helped himself to more coffee. He seemed better with the caffeine in his system, and he was like a magician when it came to finding weaknesses in even the tightest security system. With him by her side, they could do this.

"Fine. I'll think about how to gain access to the party. Once we're there, we'll have to get creative."

"I'll get to Montecito a few days early and see how much intel I can gather. You meet me there Friday and we'll do this thing."

"This is not exactly how I'd pictured spending my time when I quit the business, you know."

"But don't you miss it, even a little? Did you know I haven't worked since you left? No one has the same finesse as you, Evie darling."

Eve felt a little guilty for leaving her friend in the lurch, but she'd been content to settle into a life where she didn't have to always look over her shoulder. "You'll find someone even better than me. Or you could always find something else to do. Try going straight like me."

"Me? I'm a lifer, Evie. I thought you were, too. Honestly, what are you doing in this place?" John made a vague gesture with his hands, indicating the general vicinity. She sighed. He didn't understand.

"I'll miss the excitement, maybe, for a little while. But Deacon coming after me, making Paris too hot, was a blessing in disguise. Now that I'm away, I feel like I can start my life over, do it better this time. Maybe do something to help people instead of only helping myself." She smiled at his mock-horrified expression. "This is paradise, John. Fresh air, farmers markets, friendly people. I think I'm going to be happy here."

He wrinkled his nose. "Then my idea of paradise is very different from yours, darling. How about the high-roller suite in Monte Carlo, never having to lift a finger to work again?"

"You know I'm a terrible gambler. You go, have your fun. I'm done."

"We'll see," John said.

☙

Eve took John for a walk on the beach the next morning before he was to leave Chelsea. The sun shone as bright as a ten-carat diamond, warming the sand beneath their feet. The few humans on that stretch of sand were outnumbered by seagulls twenty to one.

Her shoulders lost some of their tension as she walked with her old friend. Over the past two days, they'd eaten and drunk and reminisced and done some planning for what she vowed would be her absolute final job the following week. They were both silent on this outing, and she enjoyed the feel of sand between her toes, the fresh ocean breeze that came and went with the waves.

When they were halfway to the jutting rocks that marked the end of Chelsea Cove, he broke the silence.

"Are you sure our shoes will be safe?"

"If they aren't, I'll buy you a new pair."

"Yes, you will. Those are vintage Gucci."

"Isn't walking barefoot so much nicer?" She'd told him to leave his shoes behind at the stairs they'd used to access the beach. He'd only agreed because he didn't want to get sand in his expensive Italian loafers.

"I suppose. I'm going to be busy for a few days, but I'll be in touch early next week so we can finalize our plans."

She sighed. "I hate that we have to do this at all."

"I know. We're backed into a corner. At least we're in it together. We'll do this, Deacon will be off our backs, and you can go back to playing house and atoning for your sins while I carry on, alone."

His voice was light, but there was a grain of truth behind his complaint.

She cuffed him on the arm, laughing a little. "I know you don't completely understand my reasons for leaving, John, but I appreciate you trying. Deacon's got it in for you, too. I won't let you down on this."

"Evie darling—" John's wheedling tone set off alarm bells in Eve's brain. "—if we're going to pull this off, an extra pair of hands might be useful."

"Sadly, my network is a little thin on this side of the world. Someone like Ivan would be perfect. I'm fairly sure he's ensconced with his sugar mama in Ibiza for the season."

"I was actually thinking of Hudson."

"Hudson Cleary?" The concept didn't compute.

"What other Hudsons do you know?"

"But he's a civilian. No, absolutely not, no. He'd be a liability. He's probably a boy scout and would call the cops or something. No." The idea of Hudson working the job with them was laughable at best.

John grinned. "He strikes me as a very reliable fellow, and he's got the hots for you. Don't tell me he wouldn't accompany you on a romantic weekend away, if you promised to make it worth his while." He waggled his eyebrows suggestively.

Eve laughed despite herself. "Don't be ridiculous."

"You don't have to tell him why, or the entire plan. The less he knows, the better. He can be your cover."

"Lie to him?" It would mean doing the one thing he'd asked her never to do.

"Call it omitting certain damaging details."

"Right."

"So you'll think about it," John persisted.

"No, I will not think about it. That's not an option."

"Fine. You're the boss."

"Fine. Where are you going, anyway?" She was anxious imagining her turning Hudson into some kind of patsy. Better to focus on John.

"Don't you worry about that. Some of us still have to work, you know."

She pushed down the feelings of guilt that had been rising through this entire conversation. She was sick of feeling guilty no matter what path she took. She thought of the manila envelope she still hadn't opened. Perhaps when this mess was cleared up, she'd be able to take that step.

"Let's go make sure your shoes haven't been ravaged by seagulls."

The look on John's face was priceless.

CB

A few hours later, Eve stood on her porch, looking down the road long after the taxi bearing John had driven out of sight. It would have been heaven to curl up with a book and a whisky, and then go to sleep and not wake until her life made a little sense.

But hard to brood when she had three boisterous workers making a racket as they finished the deck. They were working at full tilt to get the construction finished before the weekend.

Since she couldn't mope around and feel sorry for herself, she should get something done. She hadn't so much as glanced at her collection since the night she and Hudson had examined it together. With painstaking care, she finished unwrapping each precious painting, then asked the foreman to do her a favor and dismantle the crate and haul it away with him at the end of the day.

There were a dozen and a half pieces in all. It took her the entirety of the afternoon to arrange and rearrange them before she was satisfied with their distribution around the house. She found herself wondering what Hudson would say about her choice of the Degas in the downstairs powder room, or the sweet little medieval Madonna by the living room window. She'd hung countless shows at her galleries, but she still could have used his painter's eye.

It unsettled her that she thought of him so often. Her concentration was shot. She blamed it entirely on him and that kiss. Well, both kisses. The first had been dreamy, unexpectedly sensual. The second had been intensely craved, and deeply felt. If the first kiss had been the product of flirtation, the second had been born of lust; unfortunately, she was as lusty as ever.

So there she stood in her bedroom, holding the final painting up to the wall, thinking about Hudson's brain as she studied the color contrast between the still life and the room's light. When she had the final placement right, she turned her thoughts to Hudson's body, and how she'd like to sink onto her bed with him on top of her, so he could make good on the promise of those searing kisses. She felt branded by them, and no amount of wishing it away would erase that feeling.

Eve shivered. It seemed Hudson Cleary was a complication she couldn't make herself avoid. She set the painting down and grabbed her phone before she could talk herself out of it.

The length of the five rings before he answered were almost enough time for good sense to filter back through the haze of lust she'd been in all afternoon.

"What can I do for you, Eve?" His sexy bass broke through her meager defenses.

"I know you probably already have plans, since it's Friday night, but I was wondering if you wanted…dinner. To have dinner with me." Could she be more incoherent?

"I can be there in fifteen minutes. Dinner optional." His voice was deeper, rougher. Just how she liked it.

"No," she said weakly. "Only dinner."

"All right, dinner first."

"Just dinner." It sounded like she was trying to convince herself.

"Dinner," he repeated.

"Are you making fun of me?"

"A little."

"Then you can bring the wine. I'm making pork. Be here at seven." She hung up. At least, she'd gotten in the last word.

ଓ

The doorbell wasn't unexpected, but it still made Eve jump. She took a deep breath. They were having dinner, and that was it. She was being friendly. Kissing didn't even figure into the equation, because they weren't going to do any of it. Right.

She tore off the oversized T-shirt she'd put on in lieu of an apron and smoothed down her hair on the way to the front door.

He'd made an effort, which made her feel better about the hour she'd spent deciding between outfits. She'd been going for a "I'm so naturally stunning I don't even need to try" sort of look with her hair loose, her feet bare, and a simple white blouse over perfectly tailored jeans. Rubies twinkled at her ears and neck, making her feel powerful.

Hudson was also in jeans, but in place of his normal broken-in flannel, he wore a thin cashmere sweater the color of his eyes, a chocolate brown that made him look completely edible. His hair was a little damp, and he smelled like fresh laundry. The wholesome image was utterly cancelled out by the wolfish grin on his face and the bottle of Dom Pérignon in his hands.

"I didn't know what went with pork, then I remembered you said champagne is always a good idea."

"I was right." The fact that he'd listened to her, remembered her offhanded remark, then bought her one hundred and fifty dollar bubbly made her feel warm, like he'd switched on a heat lamp inside her.

She popped the cork and it seemed to pop the tension

between them, as well. He told her funny stories about his childhood in Chelsea. They didn't speak of his art, or her collection of paintings, most of which had been hung. She didn't mention John, or the task she faced. He didn't bring up the kisses they'd shared. Or the fact that they were finally alone in the house, and a staircase was all that was between them and a very large, very accommodating bed.

Hudson seemed so distracted by the meal she'd prepared that anything else, sex, art, or crime, wasn't even in the air. She didn't know whether to be proud or exasperated.

"This tenderloin is incredible!" he said, happily taking seconds. "I didn't know you were such a cook. John sort of gave me the impression...."

"That I'm hopeless in the kitchen? He's a little obsessed with technique," she said, warmed by his compliment. "I usually don't follow recipes. I put together ingredients that I think will taste good together."

"Is there anything you can't do?" He sounded perfectly serious.

Eve laughed. She was a little sad, knowing he'd probably take back every complimentary thing he ever said or felt about her if he knew exactly what kind of person she was.

"A few things." She topped off his champagne glass. "I'll get the dessert."

While she was more than competent in the kitchen, she usually left baking to the professionals. She pulled a bakery box out of the refrigerator and set it on the counter to take the chill off. The box was chock full of delicious tidbits she'd picked up earlier in the day on a mad rush around town after Hudson had accepted her invitation.

Eve had made her mind up about two things. First, she was going to sleep with Hudson Cleary. Second, she wasn't going to tell him anything he didn't need to know. The second made the first doomed to a passing fling, but perhaps that was how her life was destined to be. He was too delicious to pass up, and she'd already spent her share of willpower keeping her hands off him this long. She plated a lemon tart and a couple of chocolate éclairs and carried them back to the dining room.

"Why don't we take these...." she trailed off, leaving off the word "upstairs" when she saw Hudson was on his cell phone.

"All right, don't worry, I'll be right there." He ended the call and frowned at her. "I'm sorry, but my brother's eldest is sick and he took her to the hospital. He wants me to go over and watch his two littlest ones so his wife can join him."

"Of course." His concern was palpable. "Listen, you've had too much champagne, and I've had barely half a glass. I'll drive you over there."

"I'd appreciate it," he said.

"Give me two seconds." Eve returned to the kitchen to repack the bakery box. She balanced her purse and a sweater on top of it as they stepped outside, and she spared a moment to key in the security code, sealing the house up behind them.

"Thanks. I'll come get my car tomorrow," he said, and climbed into the passenger seat of her sedan.

The trip down the hill and into town took mere minutes. Hudson directed her to his brother's trim wood frame house in the residential area by the elementary school. All the lights were on, and she could see movement behind the practical white curtains.

He started to thank her for the ride, but she was already out of the car. She didn't intend to impose on his family, but she wanted to make sure everyone was going to be okay.

A slim, olive-skinned woman with attractively highlighted brown hair opened the door before they could knock. "Hudson, thanks for coming." Two dark-eyed children jumped up and down behind her as they caught sight of their uncle.

"This is my sister-in-law, Nancine," Hudson said. "And these are the little monkeys." He indicated the children. The kids, a boy and a girl who looked about five and three, giggled and hauled him into the house.

"Hi, I'm Eve. I drove Hudson over. What can I do to help?"

"I'm going to run over to the hospital now. Gracie, my oldest, has been sick for a couple days, but then her fever spiked and my husband and I didn't want to wait until morning to get her seen. I'd appreciate it if you could give Hudson a hand with the kids. He's great with them, but he doesn't exactly set boundaries. They should have been in bed half an hour ago, but...."

"I understand," Eve said, smiling reassuringly. "You go. We'll take care of it."

"Thanks, I have my cell phone and I'll text if we're going to be more than a couple of hours." Nancine called out, "Jordan! Caitlyn! Your Uncle Hudson is going to put you to bed now. I'll see you in the morning." She then escaped out the door.

Eve surveyed the scene. Jordan, the older one, was holding a foam football and talking nonstop about some sporting event he'd seen. Caitlyn, the toddler, was clutching a well-worn stuffed horse in one hand, and her uncle's hand in the other. Eve's heart melted a little at the sight of big, strong, commanding Hudson hand in hand with a diminutive girl in a sparkly purple tutu. He was trying to listen to his nephew while also paying attention to his niece, who was tugging at his hand and exhorting him to look at her new collection of ponies.

She caught his gaze. He smiled apologetically. Eve squared her shoulders.

"Hi guys," she said, "I'm Eve."

The chatter stopped and she was inspected by two pairs of curious eyes.

"Caitlyn, do you want to show me your ponies while your Uncle Hudson takes your brother to change into his pajamas?"

Divide and conquer, that was her plan. She held her breath, hoping she sounded more authoritative than she felt. What she knew about kids could be written on a cocktail napkin.

Caitlyn seemed to consider her offer. "Are you Uncle Hudson's girlfriend?"

"Um." She glanced at Hudson, but he looked as curious as his niece about her answer. "I'm his friend who happens to be a girl," she said, a bit lamely.

"Okay," Caitlyn said, apparently satisfied. She dropped

Hudson's hand and grabbed Eve's.

"Come on, buddy, let's go get ready for bed." He winked at Eve, and took off down the hall, listening attentively as Jordan resumed his story at full tilt.

Eve found herself dragged to the corner of the living room that had been devoted to everything a three-year-old girl could want, from a play kitchen to a dress up box overflowing with all things pink and sequined.

She sank onto her knees so she could be at Caitlyn's level as the girl introduced her to a stable's worth of ponies, from the stuffed one in her hand to the miniature purple plastic one on her play table. Eve oohed and aahed over each one, but when the introductions were over, she was somewhat at a loss.

Caitlyn turned to her. "You have pretty hair."

She choked up a little. "What a lovely compliment. You have beautiful hair, as well." Caitlyn had glossy brown curls in no semblance of order framing her chubby toddler's face.

"Thank you," the little girl said formally.

Not for the first time, but sharper than ever before, Eve felt certain that she wanted this, a chubby face looking up at her, a daughter or son she could adore with her whole heart. She had precious few outlets for her affectionate impulses at the moment; she was overflowing with the need to give love and be loved in return.

Hormones, too. She blamed hormones. Her body was getting louder with each passing year. *Get pregnant!* it seemed to scream at her every time she saw a babe in someone's arms or a family walking down the street.

Perhaps that could explain her deep carnal response to Hudson. As a physical specimen, he was flawless. He had a virility that was obviously in direct contact with her womb. Eve could all too easily picture a baby with his chocolate brown eyes, his golden brown skin. Maybe her ears. Not that Hudson didn't have fine ears, but she'd always liked her own.

This thought trend was making her a little sad. There was no baby in her future, not immediately, anyway, and especially not with Hudson. She stood up briskly. "Do you want to show me your bedroom?"

"Okay," Caitlyn said. "But I have to say goodnight to my ponies first."

Eve waited while Caitlyn said goodnight to each one in turn. The little girl then grabbed a stuffed one with the unlikely name of Joey Sparklehoof and tucked it under her arm.

Caitlyn led her down the hall. There were three bedrooms. They passed the door to an older girl's bedroom, decorated not with ponies but with cats. The Cleary girls really liked animals. The door to the master bedroom was closed, as was the door to the bathroom. Eve could hear Hudson cajoling Jordan into brushing his teeth.

Caitlyn finally arrived at the room she shared with Jordan, bunk beds taking up most of the space, clothes and toys filling the rest of the small room. Eve spied a pair of yellow and pink striped pajamas on the lower bunk bed. She handed them to Caitlyn, who began carefully changing out of the sparkly tutu and into the shirt and pants.

"Where's my mom?" Caitlyn asked.

"She had to go out, to be with your dad and your sister," Eve said.

"Gracie got sick," the little girl confided in her.

"Yes, I know. I'm sure she'll be better soon."

"I hope she gets better before the party," Caitlyn said, now pajama clad.

"What party?"

"Um, the big party," she said, as if there were any other kind.

"Oh, the big party," Eve echoed, as if that explained it. "Hey, do you want to go brush your teeth?"

"No," Caitlyn said sweetly.

"Well, you don't want your brother to be the only one with clean teeth, do you?"

"No!"

"Okay, let's go!" she said with more enthusiasm for the task than she thought possible. Parenting was the hardest thing she'd ever done, and she'd only been at it for fifteen minutes.

Caitlyn led the way.

Hudson and Jordan were coming out of the bathroom, as if on cue. "All yours, sweetie," he said. For a minute, Eve thought he was referring to her, and the endearment made her unaccountably blush. But then she realized the sweetie in question was Caitlyn, which made a lot more sense.

"Do you need help?" Eve asked. Caitlyn nodded.

"See you in a minute," Hudson said.

"See you in a minute," Jordan repeated, in imitation of his uncle.

Eve relaxed a bit as she helped Caitlyn brush her teeth. This wasn't rocket science, but it did take patience. Possibly even more patience than needed to crack a safe by touch, which took silence, discipline, and a huge capacity for patient concentration.

"All right, into bed," she said.

Jordan was ensconced in the top bunk. Hudson perched on a child-sized chair, reading aloud from *The Wind in the Willows*.

Caitlyn clambered into her own bed. Eve watched as the children, safe and secure in their world, listened to their uncle, whose deep voice took on a melodious quality as he read about the adventures of Toad and his friends. When he came to a stopping point, they were almost asleep.

"Goodnight. We'll be in the living room until your mom and dad get home," he said.

They mumbled their goodnights, and Eve eased out of the room, followed by Hudson, who switched off the room light behind him, but carefully left the door ajar and the hall light on.

He either had lots of practice babysitting his nieces and nephew, or he instinctively knew how to make a child comfortable. Either way, she was impressed.

When they got to the living room, he offered to make coffee, his invitation to stay implicit. Eve hesitated. She'd wanted the night to go in one direction, and it had ended up somewhere completely different. She didn't really want to go home to her dark empty house. But somehow, being with Hudson in this den of domesticity was even more intimate than the prospect of sharing her bed with him had been. She couldn't afford to get too close, and this was definitely straying into dangerous territory. She shook her head. Only she could see the danger in sharing coffee with a man while two children slept ten yards away.

"Sure, coffee would be great," she said.

He led her to the kitchen, where the big picture window looking onto the backyard would make the room bright and airy in the daytime.

"You seem at home here," she commented as he went about the business of brewing coffee in a well-used French press.

"Will and Nancine are my nearest family since my parents moved to Paso Robles after Stephanie died."

Eve wanted to ask him more about the sister whose premature passing coincided with his return to Chelsea, but she couldn't justify prying. "Jordan and Caitlyn are big fans of yours," she said, moving onto safer ground.

He grinned. "They're terrific kids. We have fun." He got two mugs out. "Hey, did I see you bring a bakery box in here?"

"Oh, I forgot!" She quickly retrieved it from the living room, and they each chose an éclair. As Hudson slowly squeezed the French press filter, the aroma of rich brew hit the kitchen. *It smells like home.* She corrected herself; it smelled like France, which wasn't home to her anymore.

"You were great with Caitlyn," he said.

Eve couldn't remember the last time she'd been so delighted by praise. "Thanks. I have to confess I don't have much experience with kids. But I was a little girl once, too, so...."

He smiled and handed her a generous cup. "I'm surprised. You're a natural."

Feeling suddenly shy, she mumbled her thanks and quickly bit into her éclair. The combination of chocolate, cream, and sugar was like ambrosia for her soul. The man sitting across the round kitchen table was like ambrosia for her body. She was acutely aware of how attractive he was, still wearing that brown sweater, the sleeves pushed up over his muscular forearms. There were fresh ink stains on his fingers, and his hair, which had been neatly combed when he'd arrived for dinner hours before, was tousled in such a way that practically begged her to run her hands through it. He'd been freshly shaven before, too, and his chin had acquired a sexy shadow to it. Her belly clenched and she was warm all over. Maybe the sweet éclair was making her heart race, but she couldn't stop thinking about having his mouth on hers again.

"So, have you ever thought about having kids?" he asked, causing her to choke a little on her bite of pastry and forcing all her salacious thoughts right out of her brain.

Eve considered her options for reply. She could be flippant or coy, but she noticed the steely gaze that was coming into Hudson's eyes. He'd be hurt if she didn't answer him honestly.

She decided to be candid. "That's quite the most personal question you've ever asked me, Mr. Cleary. The answer is, yes. I'd like to have kids. But the distance between the idea of having children and actually being in a position to have them seems as wide as the English Channel."

"Yes. Wanting and having are two different things."

He wasn't necessarily talking about children anymore as he appeared to be looking at her mouth. She licked her lips instinctively. She tasted chocolate, knew that he wanted more than a taste of her.

They were separated by the width of the table, and by all the secrets she held inside of her. She was only beginning to know this man, but her body had already decided to trust him. She'd told him next to nothing about herself, yet he seemed to be able to read her instinctively. The thought was unsettling. For years, her life had depended on her being unreadable, or on only letting people see the aspects of her she wanted them to. She couldn't control which parts she let Hudson glimpse. Was it frightening, or freeing?

"We don't always get what we want," she said, not very originally.

"Sometimes, we can take it." His voice was low, and his meaning unmistakable this time.

Eve wanted him more than ever by then. Every nerve she had was attuned to him. If they'd been touching, she would have given herself to him in an instant.

"I'd still like to sketch you," he said, changing the subject and leaving her disoriented for a moment.

"Oh, well. We'll see," she said, trying not to sound as utterly lost in him as she felt.

She drank another sip of coffee. It didn't seem to be perking her up. Instead, like the prey of a viper, she was mesmerized by the man sitting across from her. She swayed in her chair. Why didn't he come to her, take her into his arms like he had before? Eve pushed away thoughts of propriety, of the children sleeping down the hall.

"Has anyone ever told you that you are a very mysterious woman?" he asked, inclining his body toward her.

She smiled faintly. "You're something of a closed book, yourself."

He shook his head. "I'm private, but I'm open with those I trust and care about. You're something else."

"So you're saying I could ask you anything?" she said, deflecting, but also curious.

"That depends," he said carefully. "Should I trust you?"

At the same instant, they both turned their heads toward the noise of keys rattling in the front door's lock. Eve had been so absorbed in their minefield of a conversation she hadn't heard a car drive up. Hudson stood to clear away their plates and mugs. He set them in the sink.

"They'll want to turn in," he said.

"Yes. Let me," she said, starting the water in the sink. He nodded, and she quickly washed the dishes they'd used, pouring the dregs of the coffee down the drain and rinsing the French press as well. She heard Hudson in the living room, greeting his brother in a low voice. When she emerged from the kitchen, she saw Will disappear down the hall, his eldest child asleep in his arms. Nancine thanked Hudson in a loud whisper.

"They gave her some fluids, and she's going to be in bed for a few days, but she'll be fine. Thank you both so much."

"Of course," Hudson said. "Call me tomorrow if you need any more help with the kids."

Eve could tell he meant the offer.

"Thanks. Nice to meet you, Eve. I hope next time we get to talk more," Nancine said as she slid out of her shoes and yawned.

"Sure." Eve smiled. She found herself wanting to get to know the other woman. To be so easily accepted was touching. It made her miss her old life a little less.

Hudson's hand was on her back as they whispered their goodbyes and made their way down the path. Most of the houses on the suburban street were dark at this late hour.

She breathed in the fresh air greedily. It helped her head clear from all the coffee and sexual tension. She offered to drive Hudson home, already having decided to leave him at the doorstep. She wouldn't even get out of the car.

He directed her to the east end of town, away from the beach. He lived in a sparsely built neighborhood of Craftsman homes. The one he told her to stop in front of was large, but more run down compared to the others on the street.

"Is this where your studio is?" Eve asked.

"Yes, when I moved back to the area I was in a hurry for a studio. This house had a large sunroom in the back that I adapted. Good morning light. Not that it's done me much good lately."

Eve heard a tired resignation in his voice that she longed to soothe.

"I kind of figured you for a beach person."

"I'd love to live closer to the water," he said. "Or someplace with a view. I thought I wanted a place with few distractions."

My place has a view, she wanted to say. As he moved to get out of the car, she girded herself to be strong, to rebuff his coming invitation.

"Well, thanks again for the ride, for dinner, and for helping me with the kids and everything."

"Of course," she said.

"I'll come get the truck in the morning. Goodnight." Then he was gone, the door shut firmly behind him. He was inside the house before Eve recovered enough to put the car in drive and make a U-turn to head west toward her place.

"Goodnight yourself," she muttered peevishly. All that sexual tension, all that intimate talk, and not even a kiss. She didn't have the right to be grumpy because she'd been denied the opportunity to tell him no.

That didn't stop her from grumping all the way home.

Chapter Eight

When Eve woke up Saturday morning, Hudson's truck had already vanished from her driveway; he must have caught a ride as soon as he was able. She didn't know what to think about that, but it saved her from having to navigate yet another fraught encounter with him. She couldn't keep her footing around him. Not having to see him was a relief. Really. She could ignore the empty feeling he'd left her with last night and try to fill it with shopping for table linens online.

She hadn't heard from John, either, but he was liable to pop in and out without warning, so she didn't dwell on his radio silence. It gave her a chance to consider Deacon and the difficult position he'd put her in.

She had two options. Even though she'd told John that she'd do what Deacon wanted, she could ignore his attempt to blackmail her into stealing a ten million dollar painting, and take her chances that he wouldn't retaliate somehow. That was the option most appealing on principle. She didn't owe the odious man anything, and his presumptive backing her into a corner and forcing her to make a dangerous move for a high-profile painting to settle some imagined debt was irritating in the extreme.

The second option was to appear to go along with his plan,

buy herself some time, and then try to subvert him, best him at his own game, so she'd regain the upper hand and be rid of him for good. That was the outcome she'd most like to see, but unfortunately, with Deacon's deadline a few days away, she didn't have any concrete idea of how to do it.

Hudson's staying away was a good thing, she told herself as she scrubbed the tile in her downstairs powder room when she'd run out of things to order online. Cleaning cleared her head and allowed her to think. She needed to be occupied with Deacon and that damned painting, not with Hudson and his mouth or the fact that he'd left her hanging on Friday night, even if he didn't know it.

She was mildly worried about Will and Nancine's little girl. Perhaps she'd grown sicker and that was why Hudson hadn't called. Not that he'd said he'd call. Still, she'd sort of expected *something*, considering they'd had what some normal people might call a date. She'd cooked for him, for goodness' sake.

She was getting herself all worked up, and over the wrong issue. Deacon posed a much greater threat to her than some guy not calling to say hello.

Eve sighed and moved her cleaning materials to the guest bath. There was a lot of tile in there.

ぞ

Sunday morning, Eve rose at dawn and went out to inspect her new back deck, which was officially open for business. She was pleased with the work the carpenters had done. Sturdy yet elegant. The clean smell of fresh sawdust made her itch to get some outdoor furniture as soon as possible.

So she drove thirty miles down the coast to the nearest big box hardware store, ordered enough deck tables, chairs, and umbrellas to host a small wedding, and while she was at it, loaded up on pots, plants, fertilizer, and other goodies. She intended to hire a professional to landscape the front and back of the house, but she could handle a few geraniums in pots.

She'd gotten an early enough start so it was not yet noon when she arrived back at the house, groceries added to her haul. The house phone was ringing as she pushed open the front door. Since John was the only one who had that number, she ran for it, leaving bags strewn behind her.

"You're out of breath," John observed when she answered. "I'm not interrupting anything, am I?"

She mentally stuck her tongue out at him. "I was running errands, what's up? Are you okay? Where are you?"

"I'm fine. I'm in Santa Barbara. I have news for you, from Deacon. Is this a secure line?"

"Who knows? I would have thought so, until you came by with your cheerful news. Let's assume Deacon is the only one who would care to listen to my conversations."

"All right. Well, to be brief, he's assuming you're going to go through with his, ah, request, and has provided a few more details."

"Wonderful. How helpful."

"I know you're not eager to do this job, Evie darling, but we really don't have much choice," John said mildly.

"Ugh. I'm so sick of this entire mess. The quicker we do it and Deacon can be out of my life, the better."

"Then write this down...."

ೞ

Hudson steered his truck up Eve's hill. He was a happy man. He'd spent Father's Day morning eating more than his share of pancakes and bacon at Will and Nancine's. His father and mother had come down from Paso Robles and they'd made a full house. Gracie's fever was gone, and though she'd been lying in a nest of blankets on the couch when he got there, her mood was good and it didn't look like either of the other kids was getting sick.

How lucky he was to have family living five minutes down the road, people he loved and cared about. His little brother was the consummate family man, running his own business, providing for his wife and kids. Nancine was a great mom, firm but loving, and she worked part time at the elementary school library. He'd been slowly working up to it for a while, but Hudson was firmly in the camp of wanting what they had. Not that he necessarily wanted to stay in Chelsea forever. He wanted all of the joy, and the responsibility, that came with settling down with a partner for life.

Nancine had grilled him, naturally, about Eve. He'd grinned, and said, truthfully, that there wasn't much to tell. She was a friend, one he hoped might be more. His sister-in-law had seemed satisfied with that explanation and told him she'd liked the woman on sight, even if she was "annoyingly drop-dead gorgeous."

Hudson agreed with the statement. He found Eve gorgeous *and* annoying. Saturday, after his monthly stint helping out at the library book sale, he'd tried to channel sexual frustration into some work in his studio, but he wanted the real thing. Eve belonged in his bed and in front of his easel. She turned him rock hard with a mere glance; with chocolate from that éclair glazing those sweet lips, he'd been ready to take her on the kitchen table he'd been eating his pancakes at.

As much as he wanted her body, he needed to know more about what was going on in that brain of hers. She held a lot back from him, and he needed to know what that baggage was before he got in too deep.

He made a noise of disgust as the roof of her tidy Victorian appeared over the crest of Oak Grove Hill. *In too deep.* What would he call thinking about marriage and family, stupid grin on his face, as he was driving toward said woman? Complications were already piled hip high, and the worst part was, he didn't even know what kind of trouble would plant a beautiful, mysterious woman in his backyard to tease him with the end of his artist's block, but with enough secrets standing in the way to ensure nothing could be resolved with the one solution he could think of—taking Eve to bed and letting the chips fall.

He wouldn't over think that. If it happened, it happened. For the moment, he just wanted to see her face.

Hudson was pleased to see Eve's car in her driveway, but his pulse quickened with a shot of nervous adrenaline when he found the trunk of her car, as well as the front door to the house, standing wide open. He walked up slowly, noting the bags of groceries on the threshold. He palmed his cell phone, ready to call his brother should something be amiss. Eve wouldn't leave her house standing open, the alarm uselessly unengaged. If there was one thing he knew about her, she was meticulous about security.

He entered the house. He hadn't seen another car, so a visitor was unlikely, but there were many places an intruder could park hidden from the road and then walk in if they didn't want to be seen.

From the living room, he heard her.

"I can be in position on Friday afternoon, once I figure out how to get us in at the gala."

Hudson relaxed. She was on the phone. He started to go farther into the house, to alert her to his presence, but stopped at her next words.

"Why on Earth would I invite Hudson into this mess?" A pause. "You're crazy. I told you the last thing I need to worry about is a civilian while I'm trying to steal a painting worth...I know, at least the Mondrian is small."

She wasn't serious, was she? Her voice was normal, as if she was discussing the weather, but her words were out of *The Thomas Crown Affair* or something.

"Let's decide later. Can you make it back up here with the specs, or can we risk email? Okay. Some of my gear is in San Francisco, though I do have my gun, but...."

What the hell was going on? He barged into the kitchen, intent on finding out.

She fumbled with the phone when she saw him, but she was cool under pressure, he had to admit. She changed her tone to an even calmer, more solicitous one, probably to signal to the person on the other end of the line that she had company.

"Of course. I have to go now. Thanks for calling." She hung up as if everything was ordinary. "Hello."

He thought he was too angry to speak, but he managed to growl a greeting.

"What brings you by?" she asked brightly. "I was bringing in my groceries when I got a phone call. I have flats and flats of impatiens and geraniums in the car."

"You know I overheard you," he said, ignoring her attempts to smooth things over.

"I don't know what you think you overheard—"

"I heard things about stealing paintings and Mondrians and guns, for God's sake," Hudson barked. He couldn't remember the last time he was this angry.

"Oh."

She tucked her hair behind her ears and put on a placating smile, but he wasn't about to be handed a load of bullshit. He'd suspected there was something off about her, and he finally had the leverage to find out what she was hiding.

"Don't even try. I want to know what is going on, what you are involved in, who the hell you are. Guns and stealing and Cézanne masterpieces in your bedroom!"

"I'd hardly call it a masterpiece. One of his better from the period, but—"

"God damn it, Eve!"

"Let's bring in—"

"Screw the impatiens."

"I won't have ice cream melting all over my beautiful hardwood," she shot back. She strode past him, defying him with every step. Buying herself some time.

He kept within five feet of her at all times, grudgingly helping her carry in what seemed like a hundred grocery bags to the kitchen, following her when she went out to lock the car, then handing her the perishable items to stow in the refrigerator once back in. They were both silent as they acted out the domestic scene. He had a feeling she was trying to figure out what lies she could tell him to make him go away. He wasn't going to let her off the hook, and he'd play house with her all day—and all night—if that's what it took to get her to confide in him.

Finally, Eve gestured for him to take a seat at the kitchen bar. She filled her electric teakettle, got out mugs and a teapot and Rue's honey. The gentle hissing of the water coming to boil faded to the background as she spoke.

"I know what you heard sounds suspicious. I was talking with John. He and I used to work together, until I retired."

She tried to make it sound normal, like they'd been colleagues at a bank. Of course, no bank employee retired when they were as young as Eve. Unless they'd been very naughty.

"What exactly did you do when you were working together?" Hudson tried to remain calm, waiting for her to volunteer the information when he felt like shaking it out of her.

"Maybe I should go back a little," she started. "When I first moved to Paris, I met John's father. He was a customer at the gallery I worked at. I was an errand girl being paid a pittance to take abuse from all the curators. And Mr. Norton introduced to me to John, and John taught me the business."

"The business of what?" His patience was at its breaking point.

"He taught me how to be an art thief."

Chapter Nine

"John's father was a great thief and a brilliant forger in his own right. He taught John the business, and then John taught me. He was my partner. We only did a few jobs a year, always in different locations, always with a slightly different MO so the authorities wouldn't connect all our crimes. Patterns get you caught. We did not want to get caught."

Hudson tried to focus on her words and not the buzzing in his ears. He'd suspected she could have been involved in something illegal, but it was a bit surreal to hear her admit to it. "I take it from the Cézanne and the Rembrandt that you were good at it." He kept his voice even.

She smiled a little. "Over the years, I got better. We found a willing market in some Chinese businessmen we met in Italy. Finding buyers is really the art in art theft. Stealing something worth millions is one thing, any criminal with half a brain for planning can do it, but finding a way to turn it into cash is another. Once we had steady buyers, our profit margin went way up."

Hudson's brain was racing. "So you did it for the money?"

Eve hesitated over the teakettle. She appeared to be considering the question honestly. "No, I wouldn't say that. I know it sounds naïve, but at first I thought I was doing something good. Or, at least, if not good, then not bad." She smiled and gestured with her hand palm up, as if inviting him to understand her point of view. "John and his father came along when I had no one in the world, and I would have latched on to anyone who showed me the slightest interest. In my position at the gallery, I was of some use to them, and when they saw that I was a quick study with nothing to lose, they brought me into their world. After a while, I found I liked it, the challenge of setting up a complicated heist, the rush of pulling it off, the feeling of holding something priceless in your hands. The compensation was very, very good. John and I split our profits down the middle, though I fear his have been mostly frittered away on bad investments."

"And you put your profits into your paintings," Hudson surmised. "Or did you steal those, too?"

"A little of both," she admitted. "Some I took in trade. Great art holds its value and is lovely to look at in the meantime. I can always sell something if I need the money."

He was bursting with questions, but didn't know where to start. Eve, his mysterious, sexy Eve, was a criminal. The implications of this were only beginning to unfold in his mind. If he was smart, he'd stop her there and leave forever. But the idea that she was still involved with the life, that she might be in some kind of danger, had him rooted to the floor.

"You talk like it's all in the past, but that phone call...."

She poured the hot water from the kettle to the pot. Steam drifted out and Hudson barely registered the delicate scent of chamomile as his brain worked to process everything he was hearing.

"High-end art theft is a small world. Even though John and I kept to ourselves, you still hear about others in the same line of work. We worked on spec, identifying the pieces we wanted to take, betting that we could find a buyer for them. Some people take commissions—a Russian oligarch wants a specific painting for his collection, he hires someone to go get it, that kind of thing. We didn't. But there was still competition. John and I worked a job to get a Chagall. We spent a year setting it up, and we got it in the end. We didn't know that another thief had plans for it. Deacon. We got there first, and he felt we'd taken something that should have been his. He's delusional, of course, but dangerous. He freelances for a very scary crime syndicate out of Naples. He seems to have a lot of contacts, even here." She shivered.

Hudson clenched his hands, furious at anyone who would frighten strong, spirited Eve.

"Anyway, long story short, he says if I can get him a painting that is going to be in Montecito next week, then he'll forget all about our misunderstanding. If I don't, he'll kill me, or, if he doesn't want the trouble, tip off the authorities and I'll never be safe in America. I told him I'm retired, but that argument didn't get very far."

He wasn't buying Eve's casual tone. Deacon scared her and he hated it. "Why did you retire?"

She took a long moment before answering. "I didn't want to get caught."

He could tell there was more to it than that, but he let it slide. He was still reeling from Eve's fantastic confession. He quietly sipped his tea as he considered everything she'd said. His initial bluster had faded somewhat and he was oddly fascinated that this slip of a woman had managed to create such a career for herself, even if stealing anything, especially art, was reprehensible. More than the shock at finding out about this side of her, he felt an overwhelming fear for her safety. He didn't want her anywhere near either the police or this menacing Deacon character. He couldn't protect her if he didn't keep her close.

"So what's the plan?"

"What do you mean?"

"The plan, you know, how are you going to steal the painting?" He spoke more calmly than he felt.

"I hardly think you need to know about that."

"John mentioned involving me. Let me help." He needed her to let him help her. He couldn't stand by and let her face the threat of prison, bodily harm, or death all alone. Somewhere between her locked front door and the Rembrandt, Eve had become his to protect, and he wouldn't let her down.

She pushed back from the bar, hands on her hips. "John was out of his mind to suggest such a thing, and you have no business being anywhere near this situation."

God, she could be stubborn. "Then why did you tell me about it?"

She goggled at him for a moment, then ignored his question. "John and I can handle it. We have to get access to a museum fundraiser where the painting is going to be displayed and take it from there. It's simple really. You're not needed."

Hudson saw his window and he went for it. "A fundraiser? Not for the Santa Barbara Art Museum?"

She was slow to respond. "Yes, actually."

His chest surged with relief that he could offer her something that might help her stay out of harm's way. "I donated a print to their charity auction. It's a joint fundraiser for the museum and for art education scholarships for low income high schoolers."

"Of course it is," she grumbled.

"Which means I have an invitation," he said. "Want to be my plus one?"

She bit her lip and crossed her arms. She wouldn't be able to turn down his perfect way in, and he'd be at her side, keeping the wolves at bay.

"It's dangerous, you'd get us all caught."

He smiled. He knew rationalizations when he heard them. She was going to cave any minute.

"You need my help," he said, moving closer. "I don't like the thought of you out there up to no good on your own." They were so close they were practically breathing the same air.

"I won't be alone," she said halfheartedly. "I'll have John."

He wasn't above playing dirty. He slid a hand around the back of her neck, stroking the soft hair that covered it like a waterfall. It took physical effort to keep from shuddering at the intense pleasure the sensation brought him. "I really don't like the thought of you out with John at some swanky party. You'll probably be dressed to the nines. High heels and everything," he murmured.

"Jealous?" she breathed.

"Very." And he kissed her.

Every cell in Eve's body screamed "finally!" as her need, as vast as an ocean, crashed against Hudson's in equal measure. Her relief over telling him the truth and not being met with condemnation, but acceptance, had quickly morphed into aggravation over his insistence he get involved and then a torrent of sexual need the minute he touched her. She'd wanted those lips for days, and she clung to him as if daring him to take them away from her.

He didn't.

All of her indecision, all of her rawness from expressing something she'd never shared with anyone before, smoothed over and fell away as they moved as one, drinking each other in. She tasted the chamomile tea, and a hint of sweetness on his bottom lip—sweeter than honey. She wanted more. She bit into that succulent bottom lip lightly, teasingly. He groaned and she bit harder. His response was to lift her up and onto his lap as he sank onto a kitchen chair. She straddled his waist, happily sinking her own soft, warm sex against his hard bulge. There were two layers of denim between them, but it didn't stop her from rubbing and feeling the sizzle of promise up and down her entire body.

They sat there, hip to hip, chest to chest, lip to lip. His hands held her close, kneading and stroking her back, her hips, her ass. Everything he did made her hotter, wetter. How quickly could she be pushed right over the edge? She was using her hands to get her fill of his thick, curly hair, grabbing it by the handful, making love to his mouth with deep, long kisses, stroking his tongue with hers. She could have died like that and been happy. Almost.

She broke the kiss. "Upstairs?" she asked breathlessly.

They both knew what she meant, and Hudson tripped in his haste to set her on her feet again and take her in that very direction. Unfortunately, the break in physical contact allowed one stray, non-sex related thought to enter her brain.

"But...."

"Don't worry, I have condoms," he said, breathing heavily, his eyes satisfyingly glassy. He wanted her, badly.

She smiled faintly, "Good to know, but not what I was worried about."

"Oh."

She tugged her hand from his and he frowned. She instantly wanted to say never mind, to go back to the closeness they had been experiencing, to erase that frown and prove to him she wasn't cold, wasn't aloof. But she didn't.

"I need to think," she said.

Hudson stepped toward her, put a hand under her chin. "You think too much." Then he kissed her again, softer, slower, and Eve thought she'd die when she pulled away from him a second time.

"I know." She might regret it later, but she refused to apologize for the frustration she was causing both of them. "I need to keep my head focused until this job is over. You should think about what I've told you, and then stay far away from me. It's dangerous to get involved with a...criminal."

He narrowed his eyes. "I thought you said you were retired. What's past is past."

His capacity for forgiveness overwhelmed her. "I am, but as you can see, it's not easy to get out. I don't want you to get tangled up, too."

"You don't need to worry about me. I can help you."

"I don't want to worry." She could see he understood what she wasn't saying. That she'd worry about him anyway.

Hudson's inquisitive, searching gaze made her achy and wistful, wondering what he was reading on her face. Most people didn't look at what was in front of them. Their obliviousness was one reason she'd been able to do what she'd done for so many years. People glanced at her and saw what she wanted them to see. Hudson had made a career out of observing and translating what he saw into color and shape and showing it to the world. What might he see in her? Someone worth redemption? Or a common criminal to pity?

She pushed the thought away. "Let's sleep on it. Separately."

"Sleep on what? Letting me help you?"

"That and...the other thing."

He thrust his hands into the pockets of his jeans like a boy denied a candy bar at the checkout line of the grocery store. "Sex," he said flatly. "All right, if that's the way you want it."

"It's the way it needs to be."

Chapter Ten

*E*ve stayed up late considering the offer Hudson had made. He'd instantly jumped in to help, brushing off the scope of her past misdeeds. He seemed willing to face whatever might happen. Brave of him, if foolhardy. He could even get her into the stupid party where she could do all the needed reconnaissance, helping to ensure the success of the mission. She was terribly tempted to take him up on it.

It wouldn't be the end of the world to have another person on the team. She mulled it over some more the next morning, leaning against the open French door and watching the thick marine layer over the ocean burned off by the June sun. It could be useful to have three people, and it would solve the problem of the party.

But the minute she started thinking about how to structure the job, she got sidetracked reliving their close call. She and Hudson had very nearly had sex. She'd wanted to, he'd wanted to. It would have been incredible. And probably muck everything up. Not that things were going so great between them. She had all but told him to stay away from her after revealing her second biggest secret in life.

He'd kissed her instead of running away. It almost seemed

like he wanted to be with her, as if he didn't care what she'd done to get herself to this place. As if he wanted to stay with her.

If he was along for the ride, she'd only be distracted.

If they stayed apart, she'd only be wondering what he was doing, worrying about him when she couldn't do anything about it.

If they didn't have sex, she'd be thinking about tearing his clothes off every time she saw him.

If they had sex, she'd be reliving that every five minutes, and probably trying to have it again. That was the way it worked.

She was definitely damned if she did, damned if she didn't.

Eve returned to the house, checking her email and her voicemail for the sixth time that morning. No word from either John or Hudson. Since Friday was the party, and their deadline for delivering the painting was Saturday at noon, they had five days to plan. She'd worked under tight timelines before, but she didn't like the way she was being maneuvered into a corner on this one, by Deacon, by John, and by Hudson.

She'd learned when trying to pick a difficult lock that if you didn't fight it, you could find the flow and lean into it, finding yourself suddenly facing an open door. She had to lean into these circumstances to make it to the other side. If she played this right, she could be out of Deacon's debt and keep everyone safe, to boot.

Resolved, she dressed in jeans and boots and retraced the route to Hudson's house before she could talk herself out of it.

His truck in the driveway was the only sign of that the old Craftsman was inhabited. Eve, in work mode, strode to the house, her decision made, her speech prepared.

It took him a couple of minutes to answer her sharp knock. When he saw her, he grunted and left the heavy wooden door open, presumably in an invitation for her to enter. He stalked through the house, and she followed, getting the impression of a tidy, if dark, interior. He looked like he hadn't gotten much sleep, and he was wearing an unlikely combination of a Giants sweatshirt covered in white paint stains, cutoff khaki shorts that were unraveling from all ends, and moccasins. Eve took the opportunity to check out his powerful legs. His attire didn't bother her, but his gloomy look did.

"Are you all right?" she asked. "Why don't I make you a cup of coffee?"

"I don't want a cup of coffee," he said.

She smoothed her smile out into a neutral expression. She'd never seen him so grouchy, and she found it entirely too endearing.

"Well, I do," she said. "I'm here to say some things, so you might as well be hospitable."

He sighed, and took a left turn from wherever in the house he'd been going.

They emerged into a small, old-fashioned kitchen, and he rummaged through a cabinet until he came up with a dusty box of instant.

"This is all I have. Or there's some tea."

She masked her horror. "Tea, please."

He turned the kettle on, and the simple motions seemed to relax him. "I don't keep coffee in the house. If I did, I'd be wired all day long. Usually, I go to Maude's, or the gas station."

Eve shuddered, then grinned. "Now I understand why you've been dropping by. You wanted some real coffee."

He looked at her sharply, and seemed to realize she was joking. "Well, you do make a mean espresso."

"Why don't we skip the tea and go into town? I'll buy you lunch. I need to talk to you."

"What time is it?"

"Eleven."

"I've got to be at the nursing home at one."

"All right." She tried to imagine Hudson looming over the nursing home residents. Was there anywhere in town he *didn't* volunteer?

He stood there, looking at her. Why wasn't he getting ready to go?

"Do you want to change your clothes?" she said

encouragingly. The forgotten teakettle clicked off, seeming to bring him back to the present.

"I've been working, or trying to. It's not going very well."

"Oh!" she said, surprised. "I'd heard...."

"That I'm a has-been?"

She widened her eyes at the note of bitter resignation in his voice. As if he would believe the worst anyone had to say about him.

"I'd heard that you weren't painting," she said neutrally. "But it's not the word in the industry. I heard it around town. To the art world, you're biding your time between exhibitions."

He made a sound of disgust. "Yeah. I'm biding my time, all right."

Confusion made her shake her head. Where was the arrogant artist who'd wanted her to sit for him? Where was the man who'd charged into her house and demanded her secrets and her body? She frowned. "Maybe this isn't such a good idea."

Hudson glanced down at himself. "You're right. Why don't I change? We can talk over some of Maude's BLATs."

"BLATs?"

"Bacon, lettuce, avocado, tomato. Make yourself at home," he said, and he disappeared back the way they came.

She sighed. He couldn't be managed. She didn't know if she liked that or hated it. A little of both. At least, she had a unique opportunity to learn something about the man. Noticing things and seeing patterns had always given her an edge in the art world, so she turned her attention to her surroundings, absorbing the little details that told her more about who Hudson was than any line of direct questioning would.

The space was cleaner than she expected, for one thing. Maybe he didn't use the kitchen that often. She peeked into the fridge. It held little more than a jar of pickles and some expired milk. Not a cook.

There was a laundry room off the back of the kitchen, and through the window in the back door, she could see the shaggy lawn, turning brown, that ended at a wooden fence that matched the house. Beyond the fence was a grove of trees. His home felt as remote as hers, though it was situated much closer to the center of town.

Eve made her way from the kitchen back to the living room. There were more personal touches here, a large oil painting of the ocean over the tidy fireplace, a cluster of framed photographs on a side table. She peered at the faces, recognizing Will and his family, little Jordan, Caitlyn, and Gracie opening gifts on Christmas morning. There was an older couple in front of a church, clearly Hudson's parents. The pretty woman had Hudson's dark features while the graying man on her arm accounted for Hudson's height and strong build. The photo that made her laugh was unmistakably Hudson, his face smooth and unlined, oversized glasses framing his brown eyes. He couldn't have been older than eighteen, and he was staring at a piece of art in a museum. She could see the canvas, but not its blurred subject. Hudson was in focus and his face shone with fierce wonder, even love, as he regarded it.

"My sister Stephanie took that photo."

His voice came from over her shoulder, making her start a little.

"It's wonderful, so evocative." She turned to him. He had dressed in jeans, sneakers and an untucked flannel shirt.

"She was a good photographer. Maybe could have been a great one." He stood next to her and touched the photo with a finger, as if handling it any further would cause him pain. "It used to remind me what I love about art, why I try to capture emotion on the canvas."

Eve held her breath. Was he sharing something about himself? She trod carefully. "Used to? What does it remind you of now?"

He shrugged. "Failing."

So they were back to one-word answers. She tried to lighten up the conversation. "I didn't know you wore glasses."

"I don't. I was going through a pretentious phase."

She laughed again. "You? Pretentious?"

"Be glad you didn't know me fifteen years ago."

"Well, you were cute, anyhow."

He rolled his eyes. Eve glanced at the last photo on the table, a candid portrait of a lovely young woman with hair the color of Hudson's and Will's.

"That must be your sister."

"She died about a year after that photo was taken."

Eve reacted to the pain that still resonated in his voice more than anything else. She went to him, pressed herself to his side. "I'm sorry. She was so young."

Hudson shifted, first into her, then away. Uncertain, she backed up a step.

"Yeah." His voice was gruff.

The moment became too intimate and she had no idea what to say. There was a long beat of silence, then he saved her by saying, "Do you want to see the rest of the house?"

A peculiar question, until she realized that he meant if she wanted to see his studio.

"Please," she simply said.

Hudson never had people in his home, much less in his studio, but Eve wasn't any acquaintance. Maybe if he let someone in, it wouldn't seem like the place where his artistic impulses went to die anymore. She'd already shared so much about herself with him, and it didn't come easily for her, either.

Showing her his studio was the only way he could think of to repay some of her trust in him, and to thank her for the many small kindnesses she continued to show him, from her amazing coffee to her unadorned sympathy.

Stephanie would have liked her. She would have said Eve was out of his league, but she would have liked her, and that thought eased some of the tightness in his chest.

He led her to the back of the house, where an old sunroom had once been. He'd expanded and turned it into another wing of the house, one built of steel and glass. The light flooded in through the enormous skylights and through the back wall, made entirely of glass. The industrial materials should have been jarring, juxtaposed with the heavy wood of the house and the backdrop of trees and mountains beyond, but instead, it felt like being out of doors, only with air conditioning and a killer sound system.

Eve was silent as she did a slow turn around the room. A drafting table sat in the middle of the large open space, pieces of paper covering it, an assortment of paint bottles, tubes, and jars on a long counter on the wall that the room shared with the house. The place was tidy. One of the two side walls was covered, floor to eleven foot ceiling, with photographs. The other held shelves of materials.

He was dying to know what she was thinking. He shuffled his feet, took his hands out of his pockets, and put them back in. He stood still when Eve stopped her survey of the room and looked him in the eyes.

"It's a remarkable space."

He could hear the hesitation in her voice. "But?"

"It's very clean," she said carefully.

"Yeah, well, it hasn't gotten much use." Was that all he was going to say? If he wasn't going to tell her everything, what had he brought her here for? He breathed deep.

She wandered over to the wall of photos. He spoke to her back.

"I'm an abstract painter." He ran a hand through his hair. "At least, I was."

"What do you mean?" She was bent over a photo, speaking absently. "You're famous for your landscape-inspired abstracts."

"When Stephanie got sick, I was in New York. I was working really hard on getting ready for a show, and I was playing hard, too. Stephanie didn't tell anyone how sick she really was. I knew she'd been in to the doctor's for tests, but I couldn't believe that my little sister could really have cancer. I guess I was in denial. I was kind of caught up in my little universe; I didn't understand how serious her condition was. Then my mom called to say that

Stephanie had taken a turn for the worse. She was dead before I could even get on a plane."

Eve was looking at him alertly now, but he averted his gaze so he didn't have to see the pity on her face. "I came out for the funeral, but I was all set to go back to New York, back to my studio, back to work on the show I had contracted for the following summer."

"I remember that show," she murmured.

"I couldn't do it. I sent what I had, and they had to be satisfied with that. I couldn't paint. All I could think about was how badly I'd failed my little sister. She lived right in town, did you know? She was a nurse. The most giving woman I ever knew."

He started pacing around the studio. "I bought this house, built this studio thinking I'd come back someday, settle down, raise my kids alongside Will's and Stephanie's. But Stephanie wasn't going to have any kids. I couldn't seem to make up for that by picking up a paintbrush."

"So you started volunteering at the hospital. And the nursing home. And the community garden."

He stopped in front of his easel, on which a small cloth-covered canvas rested. He forced himself to meet her gaze, but he didn't see any judgment in her eyes. "Yeah. I haven't painted since. Well, not until last week."

"Last week?" She didn't understand the significance until Hudson lifted the cloth off the canvas to show her. Her face stared back at her, unfinished but unmistakable. He'd painted her with a smile and shining eyes. And not her standard-issue Cheshire cat smile, but a real one, as if he'd captured the moment right after she'd opened a colorfully wrapped gift to find a puppy inside. She looked happy.

Eve didn't know what to say. The art critic inside her was fascinated by seeing Hudson Cleary's technique applied to a portrait. The same bold strokes and defined lines were there, but it was pleasantly surprising to see them create representational art.

As a woman looking at the work of a man she respected, admired, desired, she was overwhelmed, seeing herself reflected in his eyes, in the work of his hands.

The tears that welled up embarrassed her. She managed a calming breath.

"What do you think?"

She forced out a laugh. "A loaded question if I ever heard one."

He smiled. "Fair enough."

"Quite simply, it's beautiful. Surprising, yes. But beautiful. Why haven't you ever painted portraits before?"

"It's as if I never thought of it. My hands started doing their thing and my brain was only involved tangentially. For two years, my brain was in charge and my hands were frozen. They're thawing out, and this is the result."

"Well, on a professional level, it's good, Hudson, it's really good."

"Thanks."

Did she detect a hint of relief in his voice? It didn't surprise her that he'd be a little insecure after being creatively stopped up for two whole years.

"On a personal level, it's breathtaking. You made me look...."

"Happy?"

"Yes, but...soft is the word I was thinking of."

"You always try to be hard," he said. "Soft looks good on you."

"Oh." He'd stymied her the way he had the first time they met. And the second time they met. He kept coming up with ways to take her breath away and make her want him more with each second.

Why did things have to be so complicated? She wanted, desperately, to show him how soft she could be for him, for him alone.

Since things were complicated, she did the only thing she could. "Let's go get some BLATs."

Chapter Eleven

Maude's was one of those diners that had steadfastly refused to be updated at any point in the last thirty years. The neon sign in the window was missing the u, the red vinyl booths were cracked, and the floor had been mopped so many times it was amazing the checkerboard linoleum pattern hadn't been worn clean off.

After they'd ordered and had their coffees topped up, Eve watched Hudson doctor his with three sugars and a splash of cream. She must have looked incredulous, because he shrugged. "This is how I like Maude's coffee."

He'd taken her espresso straight, and the night they'd shared coffee in his brother's kitchen, he only used the cream. She never knew anyone to be so changeable when it came to caffeine delivery systems. Then again, after she tasted the diner's bitter brew, maybe she could understand.

He smiled but made no comment when she reached for the sugar packets. They were properly caffeinated, so they could get down to business. Before she could launch into her carefully prepared speech, Hudson leaned back in the booth.

"So how are we going to steal ourselves a Mondrian?"

"Not so loud!"

"I don't think there are any FBI agents in Chelsea."

"You can't be too careful."

"Sure. Sure. Tell me the deal."

He was awfully composed for a civilian. He probably imagined Cary Grant-style glamour.

"I will, if you'll let me," she ground out. When he continued to be silent, she took a calming breath and went on. "First, I appreciate your offer to help. I'm a little out of my element here, both being back in the States without my usual network, and being forced into this job. Since it wouldn't be wise to simply walk away, I have to lean into it, and that means I have to use what assets I have, and unfortunately, you're one. So, if you're still up for it, I'd like to have your help. In other words, what are you doing Friday night?"

"Helping you steal a painting." He grinned like a school kid contemplating a snow day.

"I have a few conditions."

"Of course you do," he said.

"Number one, you have to do everything I say between now and Friday without asking questions. I'm not going to ask you to do anything illegal—or at least, anything you can't plausibly deny your involvement with. However, I might have to ask you to do something you won't like, such as stay put when I need to go somewhere. I need to trust that you'll follow my directions. Otherwise, I can't keep you safe."

"I'll try."

Eve sighed. She'd have to accept that. "Fine. The second thing is, we can't have sex."

"Ever?"

Hudson looked so crestfallen that she hastened in with an awkward reassurance. "No...I mean, until this job is finished. Not that we...um, let's take that off the table right now." He quirked an eyebrow and she rushed on. "If we have sex, I have a feeling my brain will turn to mush and I won't be able to concentrate on the important stuff, like getting a deranged thief off my back, okay?" She felt her cheeks grow hot and she took a sip of Maude's awful coffee. Hudson chuckled, but she thought more in solidarity than in fun.

"I can live with those terms," he said, "and I have one of my own."

She lifted an eyebrow.

"I'll help you get into that party, I'll follow your instructions, I'll even keep my hands off of you." Eve was pleased at how disgruntled he sounded over the last item. "When it's all over, you'll model for me. One session, a few hours at most. And you have to do what I tell you. It's only fair."

She sucked in a breath. She'd been afraid he'd bring that up again. She wanted to do it, if she was really honest with herself. But saying yes was like saying they had a future together after this debacle was resolved, and that was even scarier than the prospect of Deacon's threats.

"Okay." She could figure out how to handle what she'd promised when the time came. Hudson's mouth relaxed into a smile and she lost her train of thought. *Those lips are off limits.* She cleared her throat. "Let's go over the schedule, then. I'll make sure we have all the gear we need and make the travel arrangements."

"Eve," he interrupted. "That all sounds fine and I have no doubt that you have everything beautifully arranged, but do we have to go into details now? I'm starving."

"Oh, sure." Plates loaded with sandwiches and fries arrived as if on cue. Hudson's appetite didn't seem to be affected by stress, or perhaps this all seemed like a game to him. Eve was jittery and picked at her meal. Things were moving so quickly. She'd barely processed Hudson's reasons for his artist's block when he'd stunned her with the painting of herself. He was born to make beautiful pictures with his hands, and she was thrilled to see him on the cusp of such new territory, but it scared her to be so invested in him, to be working with him side by side. Not only because she wanted to literally be physically near him, bodies entwined, but because she felt connected on a different level, souls united, fates locked, and quite simply, she couldn't believe he was meant for her. She was terrified that she would let him down.

"I have to get to the nursing home," he said. "Let's meet up later and you can give me the full download."

She should embrace his help, maybe even use his expertise, but she needed space.

"I think I'm going to go up to San Francisco for a night or two, get some things I need," she said casually. "Why don't we do it later in the week?"

"All right," he said.

They walked out to the street together, and Hudson held her arm to prevent her from walking away. "Be careful."

Eve swallowed the lump in her throat. She was way past that. "I will," she lied.

Chapter Twelve

*H*udson stuffed his phone back into his pocket and picked up the wheelbarrow handles. He guided the load of rich brown compost from the storage area to the raised vegetable beds where a handful of middle schoolers were harvesting early cherry tomatoes and watering the soon-to-be enormous zucchini plants.

"Hey, buddy, watch the green ones. Let's leave those on and we can pick them when they're ripe," he called out to a gangly boy who was indiscriminately picking anything round off the bush.

He was relieved that he'd finally heard from Eve. She'd waited until Wednesday afternoon to text him to confirm dinner at her place, where they'd go over the plan for Friday. She'd messaged him yesterday to say she was in San Francisco, and that she'd heard from John and everything was still a go. But that was it. He tried not to worry about her, but it was apparently a permanent condition. At least worrying about her safety kept his other worries at bay, like what had he been thinking telling her about Stephanie and his artist's block. He'd agonized over showing her the painting he'd done of her, but she seemed to like it, which gave him hope. Not that he'd been able to do any more work since Eve had left. Her energy seemed to be the only thing giving him the strength to paint. Which was ridiculous. He didn't really believe in the idea of a muse. Besides, she wasn't exactly clamoring for the job.

Still, they had a connection. He knew she knew it. Which was maybe why she was making herself scarce. He had to admit he appreciated her taking temptation away from him, since he'd agreed to that no sex rule. What a great idea that was turning out to be. He poured the load of compost out with so much force the wheelbarrow flipped over, too.

"Woah!" Rue, Eve's neighbor and one of the other adult volunteers, appeared and knelt to help him right the barrow. "Watch it, Hercules."

"Sorry." He didn't need to take his frustration out on defenseless gardening tools.

"One more load ought to do it," she said, waving off the apology. "Hey, I wanted to let you know that Jess and I are having a few friends over for Sunday Supper this week and I thought you might want to come. Maybe bring our mutual friend, Eve?"

"Sunday?" By Sunday, he'd have helped Eve commit at least one felony and hopefully severed her ties to her old life for good. By Sunday, maybe life would be returning to normal. Except normal was the last thing he wanted since he'd met Eve. "I'll do my best to make it."

ಸ

"And then we'll hand off the painting and head home. Barring unforeseen circumstances." Eve finished outlining the plan and pushed away the rest of her Cobb salad.

"What kind of unforeseen circumstances?" Hudson asked. He'd already finished his second portion.

"Well, that's sort of the idea. I don't know. So we stick to the plan but stay flexible."

"It's a solid plan. I can see why you were so good at this."

"Really?" Why did his compliments always blindside her?

"Well, it's the best I could come up with on such short notice. Normally, I'd have a lot more lead time than this."

"What would you do if you had more lead time?" He seemed genuinely curious.

She poured herself another half glass of wine and moved to the living room. "It depends on the kind of job. A basic smash and grab requires a little reconnaissance, maybe two weeks of staking out the locations, figuring out the weaknesses in the security system, whether it's a museum or a private home. For a switch, we had to have access to the original so we could have a duplicate made, then we had to plan a time to make the switch. Those were more delicate operations, but ultimately less dangerous." She settled into a corner of the sofa.

Hudson followed her, but took up residence a safe distance away in an armchair, leaving the entire sofa to her.

"Because the owners wouldn't know for a while that they had a copy?"

"Right. It gave us time to distance ourselves from the scene. Sometimes, they never figure it out."

"Really?"

"You have no idea how many reproductions are hanging in museums, being passed off as the real thing. Not only copies of well-known works, while the originals sit in a warehouse somewhere or in some rich guy's castle, but fakes in the style of a certain artist, which can sometimes sell for as much as a real one, if they're good enough to pass authentication. Our forger was the best."

"So, if you had the time, you'd rather make a copy of the Mondrian and somehow change the real out for the fake?"

"It's not a perfect system, but yeah, it usually keeps the heat off for a while. Also, fewer people get hurt that way. The owner of the original is none the wiser and the buyer is happy because the item isn't considered hot, and it won't raise eyebrows if he's associated with it. He tells people his is a fake, and everyone is happy."

"Then why not sell the buyer the fake and skip the hassle of stealing the painting in the first place?"

"The kind of people who want to buy real artwork are not to be trifled with. They want the originals, and they have no scruples."

"So what kind of guy is Deacon?"

"He's the worst. An ambitious thug with delusions of grandeur. He fancies himself a gentleman thief but he's really hardly more than a gopher. Unfortunately, the people he gophers for are very unpleasant, the Italian Mafia. Plus, he's kind of crazy. He's got it in his head that I owe him, and he's not rational enough to take a payoff and be done with it."

"Do you owe him?"

"Of course not! That's why this amounts to blackmail. If I don't deliver what he wants, he's going to tip off my location to Interpol. Not that he or they have a shred of evidence against me in any open investigations, but the reason I came back to America was to leave all that behind. I wanted to start over." Eve was desperate for this episode to be behind her. Then maybe she wouldn't have to keep Hudson out of reach.

"How long have you been gone?"

"Ten years."

He whistled. "You never set foot in America in all that time?"

"Once," she said. "For my father's funeral." Then she drained her wine glass and headed for the kitchen. "I'll make us some decaf and then it's time to turn in. We have to pack tomorrow and Friday is going to be a long day."

☙

Two days shy of the solstice, the sun was still in the sky when Hudson headed back down the hill. He was keyed up from the download of information he'd gotten from Eve, and from the force of will that had kept them within arm's reach of one another without touching all evening. He needed to burn off some energy with a run on the beach before he went back to his big empty house.

His brain swirled, thinking about Eve, wondering about her past. He had a hard time accepting this side of her, that she was a woman not only of mystery, but of danger. She had a very real bad guy who might kill her if she didn't get him what he wanted. She had a past that could catch up with her even in a sleepy seaside town. She'd done things, explicitly illegal things, morally wrong things, for money.

He admired that she wasn't apologetic about it. What was done was done. She had gotten out of it, was trying to start over.

He'd seen enough Hollywood movies to know how that usually turned out.

Still, he couldn't help but think that she was as much victim as perpetrator. John, as charming as he was, was clearly a born and bred criminal. It sounded to him like he'd used her from day one, planting ideas into her head about art and excitement and money that an impressionable teenager could be forgiven for buying into. Once you were in, it must be hard to get out.

He contemplated the scam John and Eve had perfected. They must have had someone talented to do the forgery of the paintings. Before he'd dropped out of the art institute, Hudson had taken a class on the art of forgery. Part history class, part technical instruction, it covered the modern history of art forgery and some of the techniques used by modern forgers to fool authenticators. The class was meant to be a fun alternative to yet another studio class, and as some of his classmates would go on to work in galleries, museums, perhaps become authenticators themselves, the information would be valuable.

Once home, dripping with sweat, he detoured to his office on the way to the shower. It took only a few taps and clicks to find an image of the Mondrian they were supposed to steal. The small canvas, about the size of his computer monitor, was an abstract geometric painting with bold colors and clean lines, what the artist himself called Neo-Plasticism, on the other end of the spectrum from Hudson's own free-flowing abstract style.

He wondered if he would be up to the challenge of reproducing it. Besides having the right canvas, the correct medium, using the right techniques to create something that would stand up to careful scrutiny and maybe even chemical testing, did he have the artistic chops to make it look like the real thing?

Not that Eve had asked him to, not that they even had the time to do it before they were supposed to steal it.

It should have bothered him how quickly he was thinking of them as a "we" and this lunatic mission as their project. He'd agreed to follow her instructions and not ask questions. He trusted her not to put him in a position that might be dangerous or illegal. She told him that the less he knew the better, because deniability was everything.

She was right on that score, so he searched for a few other artists on his computer, then deleted his search history, so it wouldn't be obvious he'd been searching for the painting in question. He was already starting to think like a criminal.

Chapter Thirteen

*I*t would take them about three hours to drive to their destination, a swanky resort hotel located less than a mile from the house that held the Mondrian. Eve had provided him with a very specific list of items to pack. Hudson marveled at her meticulousness. He wondered if she was so attentive to detail in all her endeavors, his mind rocketing to a vision of them in bed, her paying scrupulous attention to him, him driving her so crazy she had no room in her brain for details. His fantasies had been hard to tamp down this long week. As agreed, he'd refrained from putting his hands on her while they prepared for their escapade. He kept his word, always, but that didn't mean he couldn't rehearse a few scenarios for when the time came to end the ban on sex.

She'd taken the lead in every instance, telling him when to be ready so she could pick him up for the drive south. He'd offered to drive her in his pickup, but she'd politely declined.

"I might let you drive my car, though. Can you drive a stick?"

"Your car isn't a stick," he'd said.

"The one we'll be using Friday is."

There she went, being mysterious again.

He heard the car before he saw it, a throaty roar that sounded nothing like her sensible sedan. He'd been waiting, a little nervous, to tell the truth, on the front porch, his suitcase at his feet. Then a silver sports car whose shape he seemed to recognize from an old Bond movie shot around the last bend in the road and pulled into his driveway.

The sight of Eve unfolding herself from the driver's seat, wearing skintight jeans, a black leather jacket, and red driving shoes did nothing to calm his nerves, or his libido.

"You ready?" she called, lifting her sunglasses to peer at him.

He could but nod.

"Then hop in."

He hoped she wasn't paying attention to how hard he was clutching the armrest as she accelerated onto the highway at what seemed like warp speed. He glanced over, and Eve looked exhilarated. She laughed at something she saw in his face, and took her foot off the gas, notching the gear up one as she settled into a straight.

"Where did you learn to drive like that?" he asked.

"*To Catch a Thief.*"

"Ah."

She laughed again. He relaxed his grip; he was glad she was having fun.

Hudson let himself enjoy the view. With the wind at their backs and the ocean glittering to their right, they could have been two people out for a drive in one of the most spectacularly gorgeous natural settings on the planet. They could be heading to Montecito for a weekend escape; lovers who wouldn't leave their hotel room the entire time.

He shouldn't lose sight of the business they had to attend to. "Do we need to go over anything else? John's meeting us there?"

"I think so. I haven't heard from him in a couple of days. But the plan hasn't changed." She lost some of the lightness on her face. "Can we forget about all that for a little while?"

"Sure." He leaned back in his seat, happy to oblige. "Where did you acquire this death trap, and when do I get to drive?"

The smile twitched around her mouth. "I rented it in San Francisco, and it's not a death trap, it's a Lotus Evora. How about we switch in San Louis Obispo?"

"Fair enough."

"Tell me about your work at the nursing home," she said.

Eve asked questions so she wouldn't have to answer any. He'd been looking forward to having her all to himself on this car ride so she couldn't get out of answering a few about herself. He still didn't know anything about her life before she'd moved to Europe and become an international art thief. She never talked about her childhood or her family, except for that one mention of her father's funeral. He was curious.

You catch more flies with honey. "I go in two or three times a week. I spend time with the people who live there, reading to them, talking to them, helping them write letters sometimes. I've gotten to know some of them pretty well." He thought of Mrs. Sinclair and hoped her kids were going to visit this weekend.

"That's so great. Have you ever thought about doing art therapy?"

"The idea has come up once or twice. Just because I used to paint doesn't make me a qualified art therapist."

"True, but don't pretend that's all in the past."

His voice softened. "It could have been." He thought of the promise Eve made to pose for him in exchange for his help getting her into the fundraiser tonight. He intended to hold her to it. Repeatedly, if he had his way. He was dying to see how far he could crack his creative brain open, using her as a crowbar. Maybe not the prettiest metaphor, or the most selfless motive, but his art needed her. *He* needed her.

A flush stole over her cheeks. Was she thinking along the same lines as he? Maybe he could dig a little deeper.

"So why Chelsea?" he asked, finally turning the conversation around on her.

Eve pressed her lips together, but finally answered. "My father and I used to come here in the summers when I was a girl. He never took much time off from the office, but he'd always take a week in July or August. We'd rent a beach house and I'd swim and he'd read all the John Grisham thrillers he never had time for the rest of the year.

"When I got older, I wanted to go to the fashionable places, like Marin or Carmel. So we stopped coming here." She was silent for a minute. Hudson waited her out.

"I think he liked it here because it wasn't pretentious. Also, he and my mother honeymooned here. She died when I was five. Someone told me about that at his funeral. Wouldn't you have thought it would make him sad to come back?"

He took a few seconds to reply. "Maybe he felt closer to her memory there."

"We had good times there. So when I decided to move back the States, Chelsea was the first place that popped into my head."

"I'm glad," he said, a hardness forming in his chest at the idea that they might never have met.

"Me, too."

They were approaching the hotel when Eve's cell phone rang. Hudson was acquitting himself admirably in the driving department if he did say so himself as the traffic got thicker the closer they got to Montecito and the 101 narrowed to two lanes.

She glanced at the screen and accepted the call. "Hi John, we're almost—"

Hudson kept one eye on the road and the other on Eve. She'd grown very still, listening to the caller on the line.

"I understand," she said in a clipped, cool voice. "Let me talk to him. Now."

There was a pause. He had a bad feeling about whatever was happening on the other end of that phone call.

He managed to make their exit as Eve started talking again.

"John, stay safe, you promise me? I'll take care of everything. You do your part, I'll do mine. I promise."

Even though she had ceased navigating, there were signs directing him to their hotel, so he followed them. Anxiety permeated the sports car's tiny cabin.

Eve's cool voice returned. "I understand. Be there and I'll bring the painting."

She held the phone away from her ear, frozen in silence as

they drove. The pink towers of their destination appeared over a grove of palm trees. Montecito's Mediterranean climate didn't disappoint at a perfect 72 degrees with a sky as bright a blue as his eyes could handle. Eve was rigid in her seat, oblivious to their surroundings. He was scared for her; he wanted to be able to take all of this badness away and replace it with beauty, light, to keep a smile on her face always, to protect her from the evil people she'd dealt with in the past.

As they glided to a stop at the valet stand in front of the hotel, the spell seemed broken and she unfroze, swearing violently and startling a poor valet who looked about twelve years old. She threw open the door to her car, grabbed her purse and phone, and waited impatiently for Hudson to turn over the keys.

He pulled her in close as they approached the lobby. "What's wrong? Talk to me."

"Deacon has John."

"What do you mean?"

"He's got him. Locked up. Holding him as insurance to make sure I get the painting."

"Fuck."

"The man is insane, Hudson. John tried to sound calm on the phone, Deacon let me talk to him, at least, but I could tell he was scared. Who knows what Deacon might do, even if I can get the painting? This is all my fault."

"Hey, John's going to be fine. You have a job to do, and I'm going to help you do it."

"This makes things more complicated. John was going to be my driver when we go back for the painting tonight."

"Then let me take over for John. We can get Deacon what he wants and then it will be over."

"You would do that?"

"Eve, you don't always have to do everything alone."

She didn't answer, but pasted what Hudson knew was her fake society smile on her face to greet the concierge.

They were silent on the way to their room. A king-sized bed

was the main feature of the beautifully appointed one-bedroom suite. Hudson hadn't exactly envisioned the sleeping arrangements. The only agreement in place was the no-sex rule, but the invisible rope that had bound them together since they met was growing shorter by the hour.

Even with the danger they faced, and his ambivalence about what it all meant, he'd still existed in a state of semi-arousal all day, the throb of the car's engine stoking his need for the woman who always seemed out of reach. Everything about her made him regress to a caveman version of himself where things like propriety and decorum went out the window and were replaced by the intense need to claim, to devour, to mate with the object of his desire. Eve. She was the first woman who'd reached him on so many levels. She made him look at things a different way, stoked his creativity. She made him laugh. She was a goddess to look at, a dream to touch. He felt protective of her in a way that was both selfless and selfish. He needed her in his life, even after their brief acquaintance. He would not feel complete until he could claim her on the most intimate of levels, until he knew what it looked like and felt like and tasted like when he was buried inside her and she was climaxing beneath him.

The damn bed seemed to mock him and his futile thoughts.

Eve plopped down her suitcase. "I'm going to freshen up." She sailed into the bathroom.

His fantasy came to life when she emerged a few minutes later, clad in a short wine-colored robe that showed off her slender legs and accentuated the curves of her glorious breasts.

"Hudson." Her voice held a hesitancy that her body seemed not to share. "Would you...be with me?"

Eve was this close to a meltdown. Her emotions had taken more abuse in the last week than in the entire decade before that, and it hadn't exactly been an easy ten years.

The news about John had been the final hit. Why did everyone she love seem to come to harm because of her? The pattern was repeating itself with Hudson. He was a good man, an honest one, and she was turning him into an accomplice to a crime he must abhor, putting him in Deacon's path, when that was the last thing she wished for him. But it had been impossible to stay away from him, to keep him out of her life. She was falling for him, and she needed him with her more than she needed to know he was safe. She'd always been selfish, and it seemed she couldn't stop.

So when they'd arrived at the room, she'd reached a decision. Why put off what they were both aching to do? They might not get another chance, and she craved the oblivion that giving in to her desires would bring.

She had a moment of self-doubt. He still wanted her, didn't he? She could pretend to be the cool sophisticate, but she didn't want to be that person with Hudson anymore.

So when she asked, "Would you...be with me?", his momentary stillness almost killed her. Then he rushed toward her, his hands, his lips, his body covering hers with all the desperation that a woman could hope for, and she let herself go.

Their pent-up desire bubbled over in a frenzy at first, making every touch and kiss hot and needy.

Then some girlish, sixteen-year-old part of her squealed in her head. *You're going to have sex with Hudson Cleary!* She shuddered all over, pulling away from the man in order to collect herself.

She lay back on that enormous bed, the beautiful bedding a luxurious cushion for her silk-clad body. She took in every detail of Hudson's face, from the chiseled planes of his cheekbones to the seductive curl of his lip. He was stretched to his breaking point; it wouldn't take much to send him over. She wanted to go there with him, but she wanted to explore first. This might be the only time they would be together in such a way, so she wanted to remember every caress, every sigh. She parted her lips, and he let out a ragged breath.

"Eve, sweetheart. I'm with you."

The endearment melted the rest of her heart into a puddle of longing. Sating her hunger for him seemed within her grasp, at last.

She reached for him, but Fate was cruel. A sharp knock on the door had them both locked in place.

"Delivery!" someone said and knocked again.

Eve swore as colorfully as she knew how. Hudson bellowed, "Go away!", which made her smile.

"You have to sign for it," came the voice. Hudson stalked over to the door, as put out as she, but she stopped him.

"It might be one of Deacon's thugs," she said. "Let me look."

She put an eye to the peephole. A tiny uniformed woman and a room service cart stood alone in the hall. Eve drew her revolver from her handbag and flipped off the safety, then held it behind her back. She opened the door slowly.

"Room service delivery. Champagne and caviar compliments of a Mr. Mondrian."

Eve glanced up and down the hallway, then indicated for the woman to enter. She left the cart and had Eve sign the check before disappearing.

Eve breathed out and stowed the gun safely away before inspecting their gift. There was indeed an ice bucket with a vintage bottle of champagne, a lovely plate of caviar, cheeses, and fruits, and in the middle, an envelope with her name on it.

"I'd never thought champagne would be such a mood killer," she said dryly, slicing open the envelope with a knife from the tray. Its entire content was a photo printed on regular printer paper with a few words typed on it.

"What's this all about?" Hudson asked. He'd apparently resigned himself to the moment being over sex-wise, and he'd chosen a seat across the room from her.

She held the paper up. The photo showed John tied to a chair, an ugly bruise on his cheek. The typed words read, "Get it for me or he dies."

"It's not the threat so much as the implication that he knows exactly where we are," she explained. "He knows we're staying here, probably knows our room number and could get in here without breaking a sweat. We're not safe, but we're also not in danger until we deliver what he wants. He needs us for that."

She was trying to be strong, but the stress was taking its toll. Her hands shook as she put down the note. Hudson was at her side in an instant.

"Hey," he said, stroking her arm. "We're going to figure this out. John will be okay." He glanced at the room service tray. "It's too bad, though. I'm a sucker for caviar."

She'd nearly been in tears, but she laughed. "It's probably safe to eat. But it would feel wrong. Let's order some for ourselves, shall we?"

"Make mine caviar with a steak chaser."

Chapter Fourteen

The art museum's fundraiser gala was being held at the Montecito mansion of dot com billionaire Jim Kwan. Oprah and Elton John were his closest neighbors. Needless to say, security was tight.

Eve tapped her fingers on the Evora's center console. Hudson was supposed to be on the guest list, with an anonymous plus one, but her nerves were spread thin over so many worries, she was liable to snap over the next crisis, which was basically guaranteed.

Even though her desire to keep him out of harm's way was one of her most fervent wishes, she did feel better knowing Hudson was at her side as they slid up to the valet stand in front of the enormous Italianate mansion.

She noted the other couples emerging from the cars in front of them and exhaled. She fit in wearing an off-the-shoulder midnight blue cocktail dress, its flared bottom skimming the tops of her knees.

She moved to open the car door, but a touch on her arm had her turning to Hudson.

He squeezed her arm briefly. "It's going to be okay. I promise."

Her heart stuttered. What had she done to earn his help, his support? She was afraid to love him because, above all, she didn't deserve that. Every moment they spent together made it harder to keep that particular emotion at bay, and would make it harder to walk away when this business was finished.

"You shouldn't make promises you can't keep," she said softly.

"I always keep my promises, especially when I make them to myself," he said with a half smile.

Eve allowed herself a small smile. "Well, in that case." She leaned over to give him a peck on the cheek so he wouldn't see the tears that threatened her mascara-laden eyes.

Five minutes in, she was beginning to realize that her tried and true methods didn't work as well stateside. Here, she couldn't pretend to not understand a certain language when it suited her, and break into fluent French or Italian at will. Maybe she should have adopted a European persona. No, that would have drawn too much attention, and she didn't need that.

Perhaps she was jittery because the stakes were sky-high, but she felt that everyone in the room was staring at them as they made their way from the entrance to the crowded bar. She had to concede they may just have been staring at Hudson.

He was easily the most stunning man there; he'd been born to wear his perfectly tailored gray suit. Even though she'd strapped on four-inch heels, he still towered over her. How unfair that he was beautiful dressed to the nines as well as when wearing old jeans and a frayed flannel shirt. Tonight, his artistic layer of stubble was gone and he smelled like his aftershave, spicy and male.

If John hadn't had his life depending on her actions over the next few hours, she would have dragged Hudson back to their hotel room and had a private party for two in their gorgeous suite instead of mingling at a boring museum fundraiser. That obviously wasn't happening, so she better step up her game.

They had two objectives: to scope out the house's security, and to confirm the Mondrian's location. They would return for it later that night.

She made mental notes of the entrance alarm and was sure the entire place was wired at every window and door. Two burly security men guarded the entrance and the rear door that led from the ballroom to the rest of the house, but they were likely stationed there only for the duration of the party.

The gala was a fundraiser for the Santa Barbara Art Museum's art education program, combined with an unveiling of the Mondrian owned by Jim Kwan and that he was lending to the museum on a permanent basis. The painting was on display somewhere nearby, awaiting delivery. If she'd had more time, Eve would have easily been able to snatch it en route, or simply replaced it with a copy. This was going to be a more audacious crime, and one that would be noticed right away. Not the way she usually did things, but she didn't have much of a choice. Deacon had John, and as long as he was holding her old life over her, she would never be able to start afresh.

There was a silent auction going on around the edges of the ballroom, while a dance floor took up the center and a band played jazzy standards. Unobtrusive waiters slid by with trays of champagne and little caviar toasts.

"Now I regret all the caviar we had earlier. You'd think there'd be more substantial food. Can't this guy afford it?" Hudson grumbled as he took three toasts in one hand, earning him a swat on the arm from Eve.

"Don't be greedy. Didn't you just eat a steak?"

"What can I say? Crime works up my appetite."

She rolled her eyes. "Let's get this over with," she said under her breath. "We need to locate the painting."

Hudson nodded, took her hand, and started threading his way among the crowd. She loved the feel of his rough palm against her skin, and she wanted to feel those hands all over her body. She frowned at the mental detour she was taking and pulled away from him.

"What?" he asked. "Wrong way?"

"No. I was thinking about...my concentration is shot," she admitted.

"Thank God. Mine, too. Are you sure we can't go have a quickie in a bathroom?"

"Maybe we'd feel better," Eve said, joking, but barely.

"There it is," Hudson said.

"The bathroom?"

"No, the Mondrian."

The painting hung on the wall of a small antechamber connected to the ballroom. Eve took stock of the premises quickly, so as not to arouse the suspicions of the single guard stationed inside. There were a few other people milling around, a couple of them talking as they looked at the small canvas.

She looped her arm through Hudson's. They took a slow tour, admiring the painting, which was really quite exquisite. Eve let Hudson talk about composition and technique and she listened with half an ear as she studied the situation. There was another doorway, but where it led, she didn't know. One guard, dressed in a polyester suit, stood between the painting and the open door. He didn't appear to be packing a weapon, but he did have an earpiece, so there were probably other security men on the property. She spotted a camera in one corner, and noted the fire sprinklers set high above in the eleven-foot, carved wood ceiling.

Eve inspected the painting as closely as she dared. They were in luck, as it lay flush to the wall, with no room for a wall alarm and no wires to indicate it was rigged to any other security device. Time to test the waters. She took a sip of her champagne and started giggling, as if she were a bit tipsy. Dragging Hudson with her, she made for the unknown door, turning the knob to find it locked.

"Ma'am, that's not the way out," the guard said as she started laughing, as if she'd made a silly mistake.

"Oh dear, of course not," she said.

"Come on, sweetie, let's get you some more of those caviar things," Hudson said, as if he was used to her getting a little sloppy.

On the way out, he mouthed, "Sorry," to the guard, who

nodded and shifted back into position near the painting, his back to the locked door.

There were even more people in the main ballroom. Most were milling around, inspecting the silent auction items. Was there anything worth bidding on? It didn't matter; they were not there on vacation.

How she craved that, though. She wanted to be with Hudson, anywhere they could relax and be together and wear each other out with orgasms.

That was unlikely to ever happen. Eve drained the rest of her champagne to wash down the bitter thought.

"Let's split up for a while," she said. "I'm going to try to find out how to get to that other door. Why don't you look at the silent auction and we'll rendezvous by the exit in twenty minutes?"

"Ten four," Hudson said, with a wink.

If John wasn't God knew where with a gun to his head, she would have been having fun.

As if he knew what she was thinking, Hudson squeezed her hand before sending her off and disappearing in the crowd.

ଓ

Hudson snagged three more tiny appetizers and another glass of champagne. They might be there on a mission but that didn't mean he couldn't try to enjoy himself. He didn't think John of all people would begrudge him some caviar and bubbly.

It had been a long time since he had been to this kind of swanky soirée, filled with affluent donors who wanted to rub shoulders with people who knew art. He appreciated the fact that they were there to support the museum's art education programs. But the crowd was mostly a bunch of stuffed shirts who didn't know anything about art except the more expensive, the better it must be.

He'd thought that getting dressed up and set loose in a sea of suits and jewels would have chafed him, brought back all the stresses of his shows and schmoozing and playing the game one played when trying to be a selling artist. But it was kind of fun. He didn't miss the game; he missed having something to contribute. As much as he valued his experiences over the past two years volunteering time and energy to various causes around Chelsea, he still didn't feel like he was living the life he was meant to live. He'd been trying to live Stephanie's life, to give back a small measure of what the community had lost when they'd lost her. That felt good, but it didn't feel like him, like what *he* was meant to do.

His thoughts went to Eve, and how he'd started to get his hand back, slowly but steadily, in the days since she'd come into his life. Some long dormant sense in him was slowly waking. He could smell the paint, see the palette, envision the portrait coming alive under his brush. That was the strangest thing of all. He'd never imagined himself as a portrait painter. He was an abstract artist, pure and simple. His technique was free and open, suited to the large scale, colorful abstracts he specialized in. He could imagine painting Eve in tight, controlled strokes so he could have a better shot at capturing the essence of her on canvas. Something told him he could do it, if he let himself.

It had been terrifying to think he might never paint again, but he'd tried to come to terms with it. With the sense of a beginning out there, he was even more petrified. Yet, the more he thought about delving into a new artistic mode, the more excited he became. Stephanie would have loved it. He could paint her, too, from memory and photographs. It might be liberating to try his hand at capturing the innate goodness that his sister had embodied.

These thoughts kept him busy as he strolled down the aisles of auction items. There were the usual suspects—spa packages, dinners at fancy restaurants, surfing lessons. That one might be fun. He'd surfed a lot in his youth, but went out only occasionally lately. Did Eve surf? He wondered what she'd look like in a wetsuit, or preferably with him slowly taking the wetsuit off of her....

"Oh my god, Hudson Cleary, the last person I expected to see!"

He swiveled his head in the direction of the woman's voice. When he saw her, he placed that southern purr instantly.

"Katrina," he said, mustering up a smile. "How are you?"

"I'm divine! The question is, how are you?"

The accent matched Katrina Van Holt's looks. She was honey blonde, with curves hugged by a shimmery red dress, lips and talons painted to match. She'd been dating his agent when he lived in New York.

"I'm still kicking," he said noncommittally. Katrina was known for sharing every tidbit of news that came her way. It wouldn't do to have anything about his life making the rounds of the art circuit.

"I can see that," she said, sweeping an appreciative glance down his body. "I didn't know you were such a big supporter of the museum."

"I didn't know you were gracing the west coast with your presence."

"New York is tired. A girl needs sunshine and palm trees for a change. I'm living in L.A. What about you?"

He sidestepped the direct question with one of his own. "So I guess you and old Stewart weren't meant to be."

"Oh honey, I'm surprised you haven't heard. Stewart eloped with some twenty-two-year-old gallery assistant last year. That's when I decided a change of scene would do me good."

Hudson winced. His agent had never had good taste in women, but they'd been close once and it pained him to think he'd been so out of touch.

"Ah, I must have missed the announcement," he said, taking a step back.

Katrina moved in closer. The ballroom was crowded, but not so crowded that the "accidental" bump of her breasts against his arm could be chalked up to pushing and shoving. "Well, I'm sure I could catch you right up on everything that's been going on. Want to get out of here and buy me a drink?"

He couldn't think of anything he'd rather do less. He still had Eve's subtle perfume in his nose, and was on a mission to see her fulfill her end of their bargain. To do that, they had to get through this ridiculous trial by fire. He had other things on his mind than a gossipy flirt from his past.

As if by instinct, he turned his head to see Eve coming back into the room. She was searching the crowd, looking for him. He hoped she'd gotten what she needed so they could get the hell out of here.

"If you'll excuse me, I've got to make sure I get in my bid for the trip to Paris," he said, hoping he didn't sound as rude as he felt like being.

Katrina puckered her mouth into a pout and gave him a smacking kiss on the lips. She pressed a rectangle of cardboard into his hand. "Here's my card. Call me."

He mumbled goodbye and practically ran in the opposite direction. Eve was no longer by the doorway. She was gone.

Chapter Fifteen

Objectively, Hudson was an extremely attractive man. Women like the blonde poured into the shimmery red cocktail dress would always find a way to cross paths with him if they wanted a piece of him for themselves. Hudson clearly knew the Barbie doll, or else she wouldn't have had to witness them kissing full on the mouth. But she wasn't jealous—all right, she wasn't *very* jealous—and that bothered her. She knew Hudson well enough by now that she could tell he wasn't into the blonde and that he had in no way invited the kiss. Even though there had been nothing stated about their relationship, even though they both might deny they even had a relationship, she trusted Hudson not to screw around with another woman while he was with her. She trusted him, period. It was a struggle to keep from falling in love with him every second that she spent with him. That scared her more than anything else that had happened in the last week. Being with him meant she might be able to share some of her burden, to heal some of her old wounds. Even though she'd come to Chelsea for a fresh start, she'd done so more to heal the past than pretend it had never happened.

Now that she trusted Hudson with her life, was she brave enough to extend that trust to her heart?

She shook off the notion. Not the time for introspection. She had to act. She'd get this job finished, then examine what could be salvaged of her mess of a life.

While figuring out the layout of this wing of the mansion, she'd started formulating a plan. It would be fairly simple. She might not even need Hudson when she returned later that night to steal the painting.

They should take their leave of the party and make their preparations for the final stage of this escapade.

She tracked him down by the dance floor, where he was scanning the room. He broke into a smile when he spotted her. Warmth blossomed in her belly, and she smiled back despite her tension. She pushed the feeling away to savor later.

"Hey," he said, his eyes glinting at her approach.

Her skin tingled as he ran his gaze up and down her body. He'd commented favorably upon her ensemble back at the hotel, but with two glasses of champagne under his belt, his perusal was more intense, more purposeful. She knew what he was thinking, having seen him in action.

"Have I told you that you look stunning tonight?" he said in his sexy growl.

"No. But earlier, you said I looked beautiful."

"You're stunningly beautiful."

Eve tried not to be embarrassed about the heat creeping over her cheeks. She was a grown woman; she could take praise from anyone. From Hudson, though, the compliment was more like a come on.

He placed one large, warm hand over her hip and drew her in closer. The warmth of the flush on her cheeks deepened and seemed to spread over her entire body.

"I love this dress." He fingered the soft midnight blue fabric, a couple of fingers straying distractingly close to her ass.

"Thanks." The word came out breathy and needy. Heat radiated from her core, and even though there were probably a hundred people in their immediate vicinity, the way Hudson was looking at her made her feel like they were the only two people in the cavernous room.

They stood there for a long minute, his hand branding her hip, her skin burning up from his touch. There was something she was supposed to tell him, something they were supposed to do. It took the emcee's voice announcing the close of the silent auction for her to clear her head and remember they were not on a date, and they had more pressing agenda items than staring into each other's eyes.

She stepped back. "I need to talk to you. I think I know what we're going to do."

"Dance with me," he said as the band started playing a familiar love song.

"Hudson, we've got to talk," she said, but she didn't pull away from the pressure of his hand on her.

"So let's talk and dance. You can do two things at the same time, right?" He encircled her with his arms before she could respond.

Several other couples swirled around them, but there was plenty of room between them and the others. No danger of being overheard. Still, Eve allowed herself a few moments of swaying to the music, her frame enveloped in Hudson's strong, capable arms. She let herself enjoy the casual but confident way he moved her around the floor before she gathered her thoughts and got him up to speed.

"I think I've found a good way in and out. Getting the video cameras offline is no problem, but once I do, the clock will be ticking, so everything has to run smoothly. I don't think they'll have actual security inside the room. They might have a patrol. I'll deal with that if I have to. Once I'm inside, and the cameras are offline, it will take me about a minute to get the painting and get back outside. I was thinking you could drive me here and have the car waiting. We'll be gone before they even realize the painting is missing."

Hudson was silent. She swallowed. He probably thought she was insane.

"It sounds dangerous, Eve."

"I've faced worse."

His face took on a stern expression and he tightened his grip on her. "I'm not going to think about that right now."

Since she understood the sentiment, she nodded. She tucked her head against his chest, sure that anyone watching them would see her feelings for this man in her body language, but not caring anymore. He held her closer, and started humming along to the music.

"This will be over soon," she said, as if to convince herself. "And then we'll need to talk, for real."

"Yes."

He seemed to hold her even tighter. She didn't want the song to end. While they were swaying to the music, she could pretend that all they had to worry about was being sober enough to drive back to their hotel.

"So let's get it over with," he said, his voice no longer dreamy.

She was jarred out of her reverie. "What do you mean?"

"The painting. Let's take it now."

"Excuse me?"

"There's no time like the present." He'd stopped leading her to the rhythm of the music.

"I've heard that, but one doesn't pull off something like this on the spur of the moment."

"Why not? We've got the element of surprise."

"Once the painting is found missing, we will have a very short window in which to get the hell out of here, and people have seen us. I didn't really count on you being recognized. We need to have plausible deniability. If we have alibis, without physical evidence, then we're home free."

"Then I'll be your alibi. You can get the painting, the same way you planned as before, but you're already inside. When they start announcing the silent auction winners, everyone will be here in the ballroom. There won't be any witnesses."

"How exactly will you be my alibi?"

"Follow my lead," he said, and then he kissed her.

His lips tasted dry like champagne. She was unprepared for

the sheer physicality of the kiss, and she stumbled backward as Hudson's tongue, salty with the tang of caviar, drove into her mouth. His hands cupped her ass and squeezed her close to him. He moaned loudly. The first few seconds of shock gave way to a primitive heat and then to understanding. She leaned forward into him, matching his moan with one of her own. She could feel heads turning their way, and she reminded herself there was no need to be embarrassed. She had done crazier things in her line of work.

They clung to each other, hands roving, and then Hudson nipped her neck with his teeth. She gasped and cried out, "You animal, can't you wait until we get home?"

"I can't wait a second longer," he replied, his voice loud enough for the couples nearest them to hear clearly, his words slightly slurred.

She giggled. "Baby, we're in public!"

"Then let's go somewhere private," he returned, and manhandled her in the direction of the bathrooms. They pawed at each other with enough conspicuousness that they'd be remembered, with disgust by some, with admiration by others.

Hudson yanked her into the bathroom as they heard over the sound system that the auction results were about to be announced. The hallway outside was deserted, but he made a show of grunts and rustles for verisimilitude.

While he kept up the sound effects, Eve checked her bag to make sure she had all the necessary equipment, including her lock picks and her wireless jammer. She'd packed a revolver in there, too, but she hoped she wouldn't need to use it.

"Give me your jacket," she whispered, and Hudson shrugged out of it, giving her a chance to ogle his muscles as they rippled underneath his fine white dress shirt. "If everything goes according to plan, I'll stow the painting in the car and meet you back here."

"How long do you think it will take?"

"Five, six minutes?" Eve guessed. "If I'm not back in fifteen minutes, then things have gone south. You rejoin the party, and

I'll make my own way back to the hotel."

"I think I can keep up the charade for that long."

"I should hope so. I'm not that easy."

He smiled at her, then let out a moan as she opened the door a crack. The hallway was empty.

"Eve," he said, as she prepared to slip out. "Be careful."

"I will," she said, and kissed him lightly on the mouth.

He let out a loud sigh of ecstasy.

"Save some of that for me later." She shut the door.

The corridors were empty, but she still trod carefully. She put her hair up into a quick twist and donned Hudson's jacket. Hopefully, if anyone saw her, they wouldn't immediately recognize her as his date. Everyone was in the ballroom, listening to the winners of the auction items and awaiting a speech from the host. She found the hallway she'd scouted earlier and pulled her picks from her purse.

She'd thought Hudson was crazy when he suggested they take the painting right then, but the opportunity was tempting, and the desire to have this all behind them too great. The adrenaline would see her through and she didn't think she'd be much better prepared several hours from then.

Hudson surprised her. He couldn't approve of what she was going to do, and she couldn't fault him. Yet, once he'd agreed to help, he was completely committed. He did things like that. All the way. Whether helping her commit theft, giving up his calling to atone for some imagined sin, or making love to her, he was an all or nothing kind of guy.

She counted the doorways and came to the one she thought was right. It took her twenty nerve-racking seconds to pick the lock, but it finally snicked open. No one had come down the hall, and she didn't see any camera in this area. She had no way of knowing if the door she'd opened was wired to a security system, but she'd be tampering with the video feed momentarily anyway, which would alert the guards something was wrong.

Before she opened the door, she prayed there would be no one taking the opportunity for a quiet moment with the

Mondrian. Then she switched on the wireless jammer, which would disrupt the camera feed to the central security area.

There was no going back. She either left with the painting or in handcuffs—and John would pay the price.

She took a deep breath and swung the door open.

ങ

Hudson was sweating through his fine linen shirt. He'd never been this nervous in his life, not even right before the opening of his first solo gallery show.

He felt like a fool each time he let out a fake moan of ecstasy. Bathroom sex had seemed like a good idea at the time, but now that he was enacting it, alone, it seemed silly and way too easy to get caught.

What if Eve didn't come back and someone saw him come out of the bathroom alone? His mortification wouldn't be half as bad as his worry over Eve. She was out there by herself doing God knows what to appease some crazy art thief.

Eve was an art thief, too, he reminded himself. She'd done things that were immoral, illegal. He saw past that to the vulnerable woman she was underneath. She was trying to get away, trying to start over. She was doing this to save John from Deacon. Hudson could only hope that if—no, when—they got the painting, Deacon would be satisfied and let them all go their separate ways.

Then Eve would be truly free to start her life over, if that's what she wanted. He wondered if there would be a place for him in it.

His life had been on hold ever since Stephanie died. It had seemed like the only thing to do at the time was to sequester himself, to try to make up for the fact that he wasn't there for her when she really needed him, never mind that she hadn't told him he was needed.

The painter's block was but one symptom of a larger issue. He'd been avoiding his real life, hiding in Chelsea, putting off his career and the idea of settling down with a wife, maybe starting on the family he always assumed he'd have one day. He was thirty-four years old, and not a kid anymore. Maybe he'd used Stephanie's death as an excuse to hold onto his youth for a little bit longer.

He knew what she'd say to that. She would have cuffed him on the shoulder and demanded to know when he'd be making some more nieces and nephews for her to spoil.

Eve had shown him that life was meant to be truly lived. She might have an unorthodox way of fully living, but he couldn't argue that what they were doing right then didn't make him feel alive. Seeing her in action, in sexy cat thief mode, was beyond hot. He'd had trouble focusing on the tasks at hand tonight when her luscious body was right in front of him and the need to finally have her grew out of control.

She turned up his thermostat until his blood ran like lava through his veins.

He moaned again. This line of thinking was getting him back into character.

☙

Eve held her breath, peering into the chamber that held the painting. A middle-aged man was walking away from the wall on which the Mondrian was hung. The guard's back was to her, his head facing the main door that connected this space to the ballroom. Otherwise, the room was empty.

She had to wait for the man to leave, and hope no one else came through the door. If the video cutting out alerted backup or the guard through his earpiece before she could get to him, then she would be done for. If he turned his head ninety degrees, he'd see her in the half open doorway, and she'd be caught.

She breathed in and out, slowly, calming her racing heart. Once. Twice. Three times. As she exhaled, the middle-aged man finally stepped over the threshold out of the line of sight.

Eve wasted no time. She closed the door behind her, making

sure it stayed unlocked. She drew out her gun. Walking silently on the balls of her feet, she positioned herself behind the guard, and swung at the base of his skull. One crack and he was on the floor. Her whole body jarred at the impact, but he'd be fine in a day or two. She wanted to take his earpiece to see what the other guards were saying, but it would be one more thing she'd have to discard later, so instead she went straight to the Mondrian, lifted it off the wall, and wrapped it in Hudson's jacket. Then, hearing clapping from the ballroom as the winner of one of the auction lots was announced, she walked out the door she'd come through.

Luck was on her side, as the hallway was deserted. Instead of going left toward the bathroom and her alibi, she turned right, hoping a side door would put her in the vicinity of the car.

It took her another long minute to find a door that led outside. Again, she didn't hear any alarms as she exited through a billiards room's French doors onto a patio, but that didn't mean there weren't any. Since she carried the wireless jammer with her, by that point anyone watching the video feed from the painting room would see there was an unconscious security guard on the floor and a blank expanse of wall where a ten million dollar painting was supposed to be.

She ran across the patio and stared. Her luck had run out. All she saw was a kidney-shaped pool, a pool house, and a ring of rose bushes.

The cars must be parked on the other side of the house.

She was running out of time to get back inside, but she was afraid that if she stashed the painting on the grounds, there would be so much police presence they wouldn't be able to retrieve it before the deadline.

Eve kept moving around the perimeter of the house. She cursed the marks her high heels were making on the patches of grass she couldn't manage to avoid. There was supposed to be no physical evidence. Why had she thought this was such a great idea? She'd been underprepared for it, and she was left stuck with a hot painting in her arms.

She estimated five minutes had passed since she'd left Hudson. Ten more and he'd abandon the plan. She hoped John appreciated what she was going through for him. When she got her hands on Deacon, she might not be responsible for the consequences.

Finally, she saw cars parked on a long gravel driveway. A few valets were clustered in conversation at the far end of the drive near the front of the house, but no one else seemed to be stirring. If she could stash the painting in the Lotus, then she'd be one step closer to success.

It took her another two agonizing minutes to pick the silver sports car out of the lot and hustle up to it. She nearly dropped the painting twice, but kept it safe. She lifted the hood, slid the painting into the heat-proof, padded area she'd prepared between the hood and its foam liner, and shut it as quietly as she could.

The activity around the front of the house started to increase. There was nothing for it. She had to run.

CB

Hudson put an ear to the bathroom door and listened. The faraway murmur of commotion in the ballroom was getting louder. That was bad. It meant the painting had probably been discovered missing.

Where was Eve? By his watch, she was over five minutes later than she'd estimated she'd be, closing in on the time when he was supposed to abandon ship. Did she know that was something he had no intention of doing?

A thought occurred to him. Was she going to come back at all? Had she parked him here, out of sight, to take on all the responsibility herself? He didn't even entertain the idea that she might be setting him up, since he technically had no alibi for the time of the theft.

No. She'd come back. And if she didn't, he'd go and find her.

It took every ounce of willpower to wait the full fifteen

minutes before peeking outside the door into the hallway. He began to ease the door open, but it was yanked from his grasp and he was attacked by a disheveled pixie in a tight midnight blue dress.

Eve slammed the door behind her. "I don't think anyone saw me come in here!" she panted.

"Well, you certainly sound like you've been engaging in some party hanky-panky," he said, his profound relief at seeing her safe coming out in a dry quip.

"You look like you've been taking tea with the queen," she snapped.

He turned toward the mirror; he didn't have the appearance of someone who had just had hot bathroom sex. He was a little sweaty, but that was from nerves.

He reached up to muss his hair a little. "Is that better?"

Eve rolled her eyes, and untucked his shirt, then undid the top two—no, three—buttons. She got a tube of lipstick out of her purse, freshened her lips, then planted smacking kisses on his mouth, his neck, and hurriedly smudged them away. He could see the imprint if he looked closely.

"Too bad this is all for show," he grumbled, and she ran fingers through her hair to make it look as if she'd made an effort to make it presentable after being mussed.

"I agree," she said, with surprising vehemence.

"Okay, let's get back out there."

"Wait, aren't you going to ask how it went?"

"No. Now that I've seen you in action, I'm sure it all went according to plan." He opened the door calmly, though his nerves felt like they'd been pulled as tight as guitar strings.

Eve smiled and he had to stem a rush of pride he felt for her. She was amazing.

But they weren't home free yet.

Chapter Sixteen

The buzzing in the ballroom was not about who won the week-long stay in Paris at the Georges V.

Word had gotten around that one of the guests had tried to leave, but had been refused exit by a security guard. No one seemed to know the reason, but the host, Jim Kwan, could be seen talking with the emcee, and a uniformed police officer waited by the entrance to the ballroom. The door to the room with the Mondrian was closed.

Hudson and Eve circulated around the ballroom, to make sure they were seen by as many people as possible. He kept his arm possessively around her waist. It felt good there, and she liked the reassurance of having him right beside her as they faced this final act together.

"They aren't going to be able to keep this many important, rich people here for very long," she whispered. "They'll get a guest list and follow up later."

"So they might not even question us?"

"What will they ask? 'Did you steal the Mondrian?' If they do, say, 'no.'"

"Got it," he said. "Has anyone ever told you that you have a brilliant criminal mind?"

Eve sighed. He thought he was hilarious. "All the time."

The emcee retook the stage. "Ladies and gentlemen, sorry for the delay. We're going to finish the auction, and then there will be a word from our generous host, Jim Kwan."

Chatter rippled across the crowd. Speculation began at once. Black-clad security guards took up position at every entrance and exit.

Eve barely listened as the emcee tried to cajole the crowd into paying attention for the last two auction items.

"The winner of the fabulous week in Paris at the Georges V is...Hudson Cleary!"

There was applause, which grew louder as a few of the patrons more well-versed in contemporary art connected the winner's name to the abstract artist whose work hung in the museum's contemporary wing.

"Thank you for your generous bid, Mr. Cleary. The museum is grateful for your support. That trip will be a romantic getaway for you and someone special."

She turned to Hudson. "You bid on the Georges V?"

"Yeah. I've never been there."

"I have," she said. "It's exquisite. Their safe is very well designed."

"I don't want to know under what circumstances you know that."

"No, you don't."

"I thought maybe when this is all over, we might—"

He broke off as a young woman with a nametag that identified her as a volunteer approached him with a packet of information and a clipboard laden with forms.

"Hi, Mr. Cleary? I have the contract for your auction item. We take cash, check, or credit cards."

Eve was saved from whatever Hudson had been about to say by the flurry of paperwork. She tuned out their interaction and kept her eye on the guards, as well as on the stage, where the emcee was wrapping things up.

"The museum thanks you for your support," the girl said, handing him a file folder and taking the clipboard away with her.

Hudson put his wallet back into his pants pocket. He raised his eyebrows at Eve's expression. "What? I like to support the arts."

"You're a pushover, that's what. Shhh!" The host was taking the stage. He looked very serious.

"I apologize for the mystery, everyone," he said. "There's been an incident, and I can't go into details now, but if the police should contact you at some point, the museum and I would deeply appreciate your cooperation. Thanks for coming and supporting the Santa Barbara Art Museum's art education programming. Good night!"

The band struck up an upbeat number as he exited the stage. The crowd seemed unimpressed by the vague announcement.

Eve looked puzzled.

"What's wrong?" Hudson asked.

"Nothing, only it seems like they aren't horribly worried."

"They probably don't want a panic, or a scandal, or something. I mean, he isn't going to announce to a room full of important people that his priceless donation has vanished."

"No, but...." Eve clutched Hudson's arm. "We need to go, right now."

Chapter Seventeen

"Pull over up here," she said, indicating a dark residential street.

Hudson stopped the car and killed the headlights. He popped the hood at Eve's request and waited until she'd retrieved the painting from its secret location.

They were a mile from Kwan's house and a few miles from their hotel. They'd driven around a little while, to make sure they weren't being followed. Eve wouldn't say what had made her so worried, even though they had come away from the scene of the crime without incident. As far as he was concerned, they'd won the battle.

She handed him the painting and then climbed back in the car. A flashlight beam cut across the canvas, illuminating its bold geometric lines and fierce colors. The picture was enclosed in a deceptively simple wooden frame. Hudson knew how much frames like that cost.

Eve handled the piece carefully, turning it over, using the flashlight to illuminate the edges of the canvas nestled next to the frame. She brought it close to her face, and then swore as vehemently as she could in a whisper.

"What's wrong?" he finally asked.

She held up the back of the painting. "Smell that."

He was confused, but he brought his nose close to the frame and took a deep sniff. Wood, and something else. Turpentine.

He said as much. "So what's the big deal?"

"For one thing, the frame looks too new, and in everything I could find out about this painting, it was last reframed forty years ago. Second, that turpentine smell is all wrong. Why should a ninety-year-old painting smell of turpentine?"

"Maybe they were stored together and the painting picked up the fumes?"

"I'm afraid not. There are a few other little details, and I can't be a hundred percent certain, but I think we stole a fake."

"A fake? As in, not an original Mondrian?" He didn't understand.

"Exactly. Not the original."

"Why would a billionaire art collector donate a fake to his pet museum?"

"I don't think he planned to donate a fake. I think he had a reproduction made, fairly recently, to serve as a double for the real painting."

"Why would he do that?"

"It's done often, to appease nervous insurance companies or to address security issues or concerns over the impact of hanging fragile pieces. Sometimes, they are used for special occasions; sometimes they're what you see whenever you go to a world-class museum. You think you're looking at the original."

"No one can tell the difference?"

"Maybe one in ten thousand. What does it matter? No one is going to make a fuss if they think the Vermeer is a fake. It looks as good as the real thing. Some people say the Mona Lisa hanging in the Louvre is a reproduction and they have the real one safely under lock and key."

He whistled. "So they had a reproduction made of this painting, in case someone decided to steal it?"

"That, and to make transporting the real one easier. Any number of reasons. That's why there weren't police crawling all over that mansion as soon as the painting was found missing. All they had lost was an excellent reproduction worth about twenty grand."

"That's how much a good reproduction sells for?"

"It depends on the painting, the skill level, the circumstances. On the open market, let's say you wanted this painting for your living room. You could commission one for about that much."

"Not a bad gig," he mused.

"Of course, some paintings can take weeks or months to recreate, depending on the medium. This one was probably made in a week or so."

He hadn't been prepared for this turn of events. He supposed that was what she'd meant by unforeseen circumstances. "What does this mean?"

"It means we lost our leverage when dealing with Deacon. We didn't steal the real Mondrian. He wants the real one."

"Will he be able to tell that this isn't it?"

Eve frowned. "I'm not sure. He talks a big game, but is he capable of in-depth authentication? If I could tell after a couple of minutes, then we have to assume that he will be able to, as well."

"But he won't necessarily know that there are two paintings, so it's not like he's going to be looking that hard."

"It would be better if he had outside confirmation that we stole it. He's probably monitoring the police bandwidth, but we can't be sure what they've said on it." She spent a minute thinking. "This is bad. With the painting in hand, we at least had a bargaining chip. Now he has no reason to keep John alive."

"He still wants the Mondrian. You could get it for him."

"There's no time. Now that the fake's been stolen, security on the real one will triple. We don't even know where it is. It could be in a different city, a different state." Eve tapped the screen of her cellphone. "We have ten hours to deliver the painting or come up with something else."

"Something else?"

"Let me think," she said.

They both fell silent. Hudson could hear little but the tick of the car's engine behind their heads as it cooled off. A pair of headlights ahead of them cut through the blackness, and he moved quickly, catching Eve's chin in his hand and her lips in an openmouthed kiss.

Though his eyes were closed, he could tell that the car had passed them. It hadn't even slowed down, but he held the kiss. The tension from the evening and from not knowing exactly when he could be with Eve in all the ways he'd been fantasizing about had him craving the simple contact.

It felt so right to be with her, whatever they were doing, wherever they were. He'd come to expect Eve to introduce the unexpected into his life, and as much as he enjoyed the adrenaline of doing something crazy that he'd never done before, he loved knowing that she was with him while he was doing it. He loved knowing that she had his back and that she wanted to be with him. At least, he thought she did. She was a closed book sometimes, but he couldn't misread the way she responded to his touch, his kiss, the way she looked at him like he was an éclair she looked forward to savoring.

This kiss, like all their kisses, ended too soon. Her body slackened under his hands. She must have been exhausted from the stress of the long day.

As they eased apart, he tried to lighten the mood. "I've always wanted to do that."

"Do what?" she asked, her voice husky.

"Make out in a car to protect our cover."

She let out a laugh. "We're not on a stakeout or anything."

"True. I guess I just can't keep my hands off you, then."

"Can't you?"

"Not even a little bit," he said, dead serious.

She smiled, then yawned.

"I either need sleep or an espresso," she said. "I'm not sure which would help me better figure out this mess."

"I think we could both use some sleep, and if that doesn't work, there's always caffeine."

"I like the way you think," she said. "Let me put this back."

She hopped out of the car, and he popped the hood again.

As they drove off in the direction of their hotel, he spoke up. "You know, I've been thinking. We know the painting is a fake, but presumably Deacon doesn't or he wouldn't have sent you in there to steal it."

"Right. He probably got some bad intelligence."

"He needs the real painting to pay his debts or whatever."

"John made it seem like if Deacon didn't get the painting, he was as good as dead. Not that I know how he was going to get it out of the country. Maybe he already has a buyer in the States."

"So we need to maintain the illusion that this is the real one until we have our hands on John."

"Yes. If we have John, and Deacon thinks he has the real painting, then we should be okay. But only until he gets it authenticated or tries to sell it. Then he's going to be back and after my head."

"Not if the bad guys get to him first."

"I don't know if I can count on that happening."

"Well, let's deal with one problem at a time. First, we need to make him think we've got the real painting. So let's leak the fact that the Mondrian has been stolen."

"Leak?"

"You know, start a rumor. There are already rumors from the party ending strangely. We need to fan the fire." His voice grew animated as he warmed up to his plan.

"I see...like, tip off a reporter or something."

"Exactly. Or post something to some social media sites. If he's watching TV or online at all, then he'll see confirmation in the press."

"If they interview someone from the museum and they deny it, we're screwed."

"It's worth a shot."

Eve nodded. "You're right. It's the best plan we have so far."

"Let's make some calls."

Chapter Eighteen

*E*ve was running on three hours of sleep, two shots of espresso, and adrenaline. She'd ordered a full breakfast for the two of them, but most of the food on the room service cart sat cold and uneaten. She clicked off the mid-morning local news, which had run a two-minute story about the apparent theft of the Mondrian, though the police were staying close-lipped. The impression given by the perky redheaded reporter was that something had gone down during the swanky fundraiser at billionaire Jim Kwan's Montecito mansion, but that fear of a scandal had everyone keeping mum. It would have to be enough to convince Deacon they'd stolen the real thing.

Eve prayed Deacon was keeping up with the day's news, and that he was greedy enough to take the painting and run.

If he didn't, her backup plan was the snub-nosed revolver she'd only ever shot at the firing range.

First, she had to persuade Hudson to stay behind while she made the trade.

She took a deep breath and called out, "Hudson, I've been thinking...."

"Wait, I can't hear you," he said, emerging from the bathroom with shaving cream on his face, wearing nothing but a thick white towel wrapped around his hips. He looked like sin incarnate and she momentarily lost her train of thought.

"Um, yeah, I've been thinking that it would be best if you stayed here while I go make the trade. I'll call you the moment John and I are out of there and safe. I'll go park the Lotus in a secure lot—I can pick it up later—and rent something roomier, then come pick you up and head up north."

He stared at her. "Don't be ridiculous," he said calmly. "I'm going with you."

She kept her voice light. "I really think it would be better if I went alone."

"There is no way in Hell I am going to let you meet that Eurotrash asshole by yourself."

"Look, I appreciate all your help, but this is not your battle. The deal was you helped me get into the party. You did your part. I can't ask you to stay involved." She had trouble keeping her breathing even when she imagined Hudson being there if something terrible went down at the meet.

He apparently wasn't buying her argument. "Tough luck, because I am involved. I'm going and that's final."

"I don't want to have to watch out for my back and yours, too," she said, biting the words out, hoping he'd understand what she really meant.

"You think I'm a liability?" He sounded incredulous. "After everything we've been through together, you don't think I can handle myself?"

"Deacon could be armed, he could have backup, he could have laid a trap that we can't even imagine." Her voice was growing desperate.

"Those are all reasons why you need someone else with you. You need me with you." He started to walk back into the bathroom as if the discussion was over.

"I couldn't live with myself if anything happened to you," she cried out.

He turned to face her, the tautness gone from his face. He lifted the corner of his mouth in a gentle smile that made her heart ache.

"The feeling is mutual, sweetheart. Now, let me shave and we'll go finish this."

Eve nodded, unsmiling. She waited until she heard the water running, picked up her bag, and left the room, easing the door shut behind her.

○※

Eve double-checked the address she'd programmed into her phone. She was at a lonely agricultural intersection outside the city. She appeared to be in the right place, but Deacon was running late. All she could see were orange trees, stretching out in uniform rows like glossy green soldiers lined up for inspection. She parked, cut the engine, and popped the hood. After drawing the painting from its hiding spot, she carefully propped it, wrapped in its protective fabric, against the bonnet of the car.

Her plan was simple. Give Deacon the painting, take John, get the hell out of there. If Deacon tried to back out or tried to eliminate the witnesses, she'd defend herself. At least, she told herself she would. If he bought it, and later found out the truth, she'd deal with that when the time came. Maybe she'd go underground. She could dye her hair. Move someplace warm and tropical. Lie on the beach.

The idea of going into hiding made her feel sick to her stomach. Leaving Hudson, never seeing him again, would be worse than whatever punishment Deacon would have in store for her.

A vehicle approached from the direction of the city, a large black SUV with tinted windows. *Typical.* She prayed John was safe inside.

The SUV parked with its nose against the grill of the Lotus, blocking her in, so she'd have to reverse before she'd be able to drive away. Deacon exited the vehicle from the passenger side, as the driver, a squat man wearing a black turtleneck even though it was another gorgeous June day, took up a menacing position on the other side of the car.

Deacon, in contrast, was dressed for a day at the beach. He wore a crisp pink polo shirt, designer white shorts that probably cost more than her espresso maker, and leather sandals. To top it all off, a pair of Ray Bans perched on his prominent nose.

"Evie, I knew I could count on you," he said, in his lightly accented voice, sounding as if they were catching up at a garden party instead of transacting life or death business.

She shuddered at his use of John's nickname for her.

"I have what you want," she said.

"So I hear." He smirked. "Your little exploit is all over the news. Quite a black eye for that prick Kwan."

"You know him?" she asked, catching the note of derision in Deacon's voice.

"We used to be in business together. He thinks I owe him a great deal of money. So I decided to steal his pet, so that I could get it back for him as a favor. When I return it to him, I'm sure he'll consider the slate wiped clean."

"So you got me to do your dirty work. Classy, Deacon."

"I believe in getting the right tools for the job. You, my dear, are the best this region has to offer."

"Thanks," she said flatly. "I thought you tracked me down because of the Chagall thing?"

"Oh, no, who cares about that? I needed that Mondrian to square myself with Kwan. John told me you were in California, so I figured out how to kill two birds. Now, where is my painting?"

Eve froze. Ice encased her heart, making it difficult to breathe. *John* had told Deacon where to find her?

As she was processing this, the man himself opened the back door of the SUV and climbed out. He looked fit and grimly happy, not like a hostage.

"John?" She hated the note of bewilderment in her voice as she spoke his name.

"I'm sorry, Evie darling. I'm hard up, you see. I'm into some Hong Kong businessmen for way too much. Deacon's going to give me a fat finder's fee, and I needed to make sure you were properly motivated. I didn't want you backing out at the last minute."

"I see," she said, noticeably calmer. Her best friend had deceived her, her heart was cold enough to freeze her faith in humanity, but no one would know it from looking at her. She refused to let the harsh sting of betrayal get the better of her.

She spent a long moment studying John, whose ingratiating smile suddenly seemed as empty as their friendship had turned out to be. He had been like a brother to her for ten years, and in a few days, he'd used her and put her in danger without a second thought. She was no better than a pawn to him. Eve shook her head, any sentiment she may once have had for him turning to dust.

She spoke to Deacon, ignoring John altogether. "Here's what we're going to do. I am going to give you your precious painting. You're going to take it and do whatever you think you need to do. I am never going to hear from either of you again. If I do, or if you so much as breathe another word about me the rest of your lives, so help me, I will tell Jim Kwan what you did, and I'll help him track you down myself."

Deacon bared his piranha teeth at her, but John looked taken aback. "Really, darling, don't you understand—"

She shot back before he finished. "I'm not your darling. What I understand is that you have been using me for a decade and I'm not going to put up with it any longer. I'm not a lost, sad little girl. I don't need what you're offering."

Eve walked around the car and grabbed the painting. Before she handed it over, she paused. "Not that it's worth much, but do I have your word that today is last time I will ever set eyes on either of you?"

The men didn't rush to agree, but when she motioned that she might break the Mondrian over her knee, they both found their tongues and answered in the affirmative. She placed the canvas in Deacon's outstretched hand. He unwrapped the covering and chortled when he saw the distinctive pattern of paint on canvas.

"I almost feel bad that you aren't getting a cut. You did such a stellar job," he said.

"Believe me, never having to deal with you again is payment enough," she said, trying to keep her temper in check. "Now go."

John frowned at her. "Evie, you don't really mean that you never—"

She took out her revolver and aimed it squarely at her friend. "You can see that I'm as serious as a heart attack. Get. Out. Of. Here."

Deacon didn't have to be asked twice. He scrambled into the passenger seat, indicating to the driver to make haste. John took longer, but he went as well. "Good bye, Evie."

"Good bye, John."

Then they drove away.

Chapter Nineteen

She stood by the side of the road, a gun in her hand and tear tracks marking her beautiful face. A feeling close to terror took over Hudson's body as he sprinted out of the taxi and to her side.

"Are you all right? Are you hurt? Talk to me, sweetheart." He smoothed down her hair, used his thumbs to clear the mascara smudged under her eyes.

"I'm all right," she said mechanically.

"Are you sure?" When she nodded and her eyes finally met his, he could see she was unharmed. He crushed her to him.

"Don't ever do that again! I was out of my mind...." His words trailed off as he noticed that the two of them were alone on the country road. "Where's John? What happened?"

"I'll tell you everything. Can we go home?"

༙

Hudson kept a light grip on the steering wheel of the Lotus as he navigated the stretch of road between San Louis Obispo and Chelsea. When they passed SLO-Town, Eve started to tell him what had happened, about John's role in the entire ordeal.

He waited until she was finished before clarifying.

"So they think you stole the real painting, and they are going

...an for a finder's fee that will square both of them ...guys they owe money to."

"And you ordered them never to come near you again."

"Yes."

"How good do you suppose their word is?"

"Worth less than a wooden penny." She sighed. "They don't have the real painting, so Kwan is going to see through Deacon's little scheme. Which means Deacon has no way out, and John won't be getting whatever it is that Deacon promised him, which he probably had no intention of delivering, anyway."

"What do you suppose Kwan will do?"

"Not my problem. I hope it means they both will be in too much of a world of hurt to worry about me."

"Even though you gave them the wrong painting?" He didn't trust them not to take some sort of petty revenge on Eve, and he was afraid for her.

"I know. If Kwan leaves them alive, they might come after me for kicks."

"I don't like the sound of that."

She turned away. Acres of farmland spread like a blanket outside the car window. The world outside seemed quiet and calm. "The smart thing to do would be to leave and start over somewhere new. Again."

The possibility of her leaving slammed into him like a punch to the throat.

"I'm sick of being controlled by other people, by what I'm afraid they'll do or what I think I owe them. John showed me today that any loyalty I had to the life I was living was completely misplaced. For the past ten years, I've made decisions as a reaction against something or somebody else. I want to start making decisions for me, for my future."

Hudson held his breath.

"Which means I need to tell you not only who I am, but who I was. Because when I'm finished, you probably aren't going to want to see me anymore."

He let her speak without interrupting. He never spoke when he didn't have to, but that didn't mean he wasn't listening to every word.

"I barely remember my mother. After she died, my father loved me so much, he made having a mother irrelevant. He was always, always there for me, from parent teacher conferences to ballet recitals to picking me up from school when I got sick. He worked hard, but he never palmed me off on a nanny or a babysitter, at least not when it came to the important stuff. He never missed anything that I asked him to be there for.

"I asked him for a lot. He never said no. I think that was the problem. I should admit it—I was spoiled rotten. I always had to have my way, and he always gave it to me. I think if I had asked for anything truly outrageous, he would have said no, but if I wanted to stay up an extra hour or have two scoops of ice cream instead of one, he couldn't refuse me.

"As I grew up, I didn't realize that wasn't how the world worked. I had never had to work. I had been allowed to quit anything that I didn't like, from Girl Scouts to chemistry. I think he thought he was protecting me, but he was teaching me to be a selfish brat.

"I got into Stanford. Dad couldn't have been prouder. I'd like to think that I got in on my own merit, but I'm sure that Dad had something to do with it. Even that wasn't good enough for me. I wanted to take a gap year, travel Europe with my friends on my father's money. That was the first time he said no."

Eve drew in a ragged breath. He hated seeing her in pain, but he knew how important sharing this was, for both of them. She continued, tears rolling down her cheeks. He resisted the urge to pull over and cradle her in his arms. She had to finish this on her own.

"We had a huge fight. I couldn't understand why he wouldn't give in. He was worried about me. I can see that now. I was eighteen, traveling alone for the first time. It would have been a disaster; he was right not to let me go. Of course, that wasn't what I thought back then. I packed a bag and bought a one-way plane ticket to Paris. He didn't know I was gone until I was already in the air.

"He tracked me down at the hotel, the Georges V. The only hotel I knew. We'd stayed there at Christmas a couple of years before. He told me he was cutting off my credit card and booking me on the next plane home. I told him I hated him and I was going to stay.

"I regretted it as soon as I hung up. I'd never told him I hated him before. I didn't hate him. The worst part was I was lonely, and homesick, but I couldn't bear the idea of going home and facing the consequences. So I forced myself to wander around the city for a couple of days. He left messages, but I didn't answer them.

"Then one day I came back to the hotel after walking around, doing touristy things, hating every minute of it. There was an urgent message from my father's secretary. I was going to call her back, but the phone rang in my room the moment I walked through the door. My father had died that morning of a stroke."

"Oh, sweetheart." His heart went out to her, knowing how impossibly awful hearing about a loved one's death over the phone was, especially when you were faraway, too late to do anything, even say goodbye.

"I flew home for the funeral. I couldn't go to Stanford. I guess I was too stubborn or too selfish. I wouldn't take my allowance, either. I sold some of my jewelry and flew back to Paris. I stayed in Europe for ten years."

They'd been sitting in his driveway for the past ten minutes. With a sleeve, Eve ineffectively mopped up the tears that had been flowing. Hudson wanted to hold her more than anything, but he had to know that was what she wanted.

"So you see, I'm not only a criminal who's dumb enough to be conned by her partner and best friend, I'm a selfish bitch who killed her father and didn't even have the heart to enact what his wishes for me would have been. I'm not a good person, Hudson."

"Hush," he said, and cradled her against his chest. He stroked her hair, and said again, "hush." She sobbed into him, and he didn't let go.

His heart was breaking for the girl she had been. How alone she must have felt. Even when Stephanie died, he'd had his parents and his brother to share the grief with. He smoothed her hair, wanting to smooth away the years she'd spent filling the emptiness inside her with false friends and the thrill of the illicit.

By the time the setting sun started to stain the summer sky red, Eve's breathing finally slowed to normal. She pushed away and peeked up at him. Her eyes were red. Her makeup was long gone. She took a tissue he offered her and blew her nose soundly. He thought she was the most beautiful woman he'd ever helped commit a felony. Or was it a felony if it was a fake? It didn't seem the right time to ask.

"I should let you go in and unpack," she said.

"Do you want to come in? We could order a pizza, put on a movie." The attempt at normalcy didn't feel as...abnormal...as he thought it would.

She shook her head. "I've asked enough of you lately. I can't ask you to keep taking care of me."

He took a deep breath. How many times would he have to show her that he wasn't going anywhere before it finally sank in? The last thing he wanted after that experience was to let her go home to that lonely house on a hill.

"Okay, you don't have to ask anything of me. It's my turn to ask something of you. You owe me a modeling session. I'd like to collect."

"Now?" Her voice came out in an embarrassed squeak. "I must look like something the cat dragged in."

"You're lovely. Red looks good on you." He eased the key out of the ignition and opened his door. It felt good to get out of that tin can of a car and stretch his legs.

Eve glanced down at her black and white ensemble. "I'm not wearing red." Then she pulled down the sun visor and peered at herself in the tiny mirror. "Ugh. I'm red from crying. It's not very gentlemanly of you to point it out."

"It's not very ladylike of you to renege on our agreement. We had a deal. I get you into the party, you pose for me."

"You want me to do it now?" Her voice was clear and incredulous. It pleased him that she no longer seemed to be dwelling on the sad story she'd shared.

"Now, or after pizza and a movie. And sex. And a good night's sleep. Let's take it one step at a time, shall we?"

"One step at a time," she repeated, doubt lacing her voice.

"I promise, if you ever feel even remotely uncomfortable, you can leave and we'll consider the agreement null." He easily swung both of their bags onto his shoulders and led the way up the rest of the driveway.

He heard her scramble to follow. "Uncomfortable isn't exactly my issue. But pizza does sound good."

He hid his smile of triumph as he unlocked the front door. *Round one, Hudson Cleary.* On to round two.

Chapter Twenty

*M*aybe she was experiencing some kind of delayed posttraumatic stress thing; maybe she was completely exhausted; or maybe she'd stepped into a dreamlike parallel universe. But when she closed her eyes and opened them again, the steaming hot bubble bath was still right in front of her. Hudson had drawn it for her, placing a clean towel and a bathrobe on a hook next to the big, old-fashioned claw tub.

He'd ushered her in, told her the pizza would be there in half an hour, then left.

It took every ounce of her willpower not to burst into tears again at the sheer niceness of it all. She'd exposed him to criminals, allowed him to abet her in a crime, ditched him in a hotel room, almost, but not quite, had sex with him twice, well, three times, and told him her darkest secrets. In return, he made her a bubble bath.

The stress of the last forty-eight hours washed away as she lowered into the water and scrubbed herself clean. The bathroom was warm and cozy. He'd obviously put work into the old Craftsman, equipped it with modern touches like heated floor tiles and excellent water pressure, while retaining the impeccable workmanship of master woodworkers in every room, such as the carved wooden tiles illustrating a sunburst decorating the doorway and the single window over the sink.

Hudson had been a surprise since the moment he'd arrived at her front door with a toolbox and a gruff attitude. She couldn't peg him, couldn't anticipate when he'd be sweet or when he'd be demanding. She'd seen the impatient artist side of him on more than one occasion. She'd seen the passionate, virile man as well. And it seemed there was a sensitive side to all that stoicism and attitude. She wondered how many other women he'd drawn bubble baths for, if he was such a pro at it.

It didn't matter. She'd learned to let go of so many things. The past only got in the way of the present. She'd thought the solution to that was simply to ignore the past, but she was learning that was no way to ease its hold on her.

Hudson seemed to understand how she'd gotten to this odd place in her life, at once so far and so close to who she'd once been. He'd given her so much, and had resisted taking what she knew he wanted.

She owed him, because she'd given her word and she believed in making good. Eve would give him her body because it was hers to give as she saw fit. She'd give him her heart because she didn't have a choice.

The water cooled; the bubbles started to get patchy. She washed herself with a fragrant bar of clove-scented soap. The manliest of the scents you could get at the Chelsea drug store, it smelled like Hudson.

A tentative knock came at the door. At her "Come in!", Hudson peeked his head around the door. She didn't bother to cover herself. He'd seen most of her in bits and pieces, anyway.

"Hey, uh, the pizza's here."

She enjoyed the way his gaze stayed valiantly glued to the wall behind her head. His self-control would pay off later.

"I'll be down in two minutes," she said, smiling sweetly.

"Uh, okay," he said, and ducked away.

It took her just that long to towel off and slip on the robe he'd provided. There was no need to get into her suitcase for clean clothes yet, even though Hudson had thoughtfully placed it inside the door to the bathroom.

She found him dishing up pizza slices onto white ceramic plates in the living room. A fire snapped in a stone hearth, giving the room the feeling of a cozy winter's eve rather than a midsummer night.

"I poured us some wine," he said. "Not champagne, but this'll work with the pizza."

She curled up on one end of the couch and took a sip of the red. The peppery flavor unfolded on her tongue and she took a moment to enjoy the sensation. "It's perfect," she declared.

"It's from my mom's place. I mean, it's not her winery, but she's worked there for years."

"Really? What an interesting place to work." Then she watched Hudson devour a slice of pepperoni and black olive in two bites.

"I wasn't sure what you liked, so I got half veggie, half pepperoni."

"I like pepperoni, but I wouldn't want the veggie to go to waste," she laughed, taking a slice for herself.

"Oh, it wouldn't," he assured her.

"Well, save some room for dessert," she said in a low voice.

"What's for dessert?"

"Me."

She hummed with satisfaction when he started choking on his pepperoni. He took a glug of wine, which didn't help.

"You?" he managed to spit out.

"We had a deal, didn't we? You reminded me this evening."

"That's right."

"Well, first you can draw me, and then you can have me."

The bold statement suited the kind of sleepy, sultry mood she was in. He was a stunningly gorgeous, patently passionate artist with hands that could drive a woman mad in seconds. She wanted those hands on her, driving her mad, making her forget about everything except the heat and the pleasure. Though she'd never been an exhibitionist, there was something strangely erotic about the idea of sitting before him, where he could look but not touch, letting him turn her body into art with those clever fingers.

Apparently, he thought so, too, because she'd never seen him move so quickly. He slapped the lid on the pizza box closed. "I'm finished."

She laughed. "Well, I'm not, so slow down. We have all night."

"I like the sound of that." He met her eyes across the coffee table and poured them both more wine.

"Tell me more about your parents," she said, turning the conversation away from lust before she melted.

"All right. My dad's retired, my mom still pours for the tourists most weekends. High school sweethearts, married forty years. My dad inherited the locksmith business from his father, a German immigrant who arrived right before World War I broke out. He landed in New York, and thought anyone who stayed there was out of his mind. He kept pushing west until he couldn't get any farther. He married a Mexican girl, and my mom's family goes way back to the California rancheros, so I've got a bit of American Indian, Spanish, Mexican, you name it, in me."

"You're the oldest, right?" she asked, topping up their glasses.

"Yeah. Stephanie came along two years after me. She was always their favorite. Will's the baby, and he made my dad so happy by taking over the family business. I thought he was crazy, but he's done really well with it, expanded the scope. It suits him. I'm the odd one out."

Hudson didn't seem to realize how lucky he was to have a family at all.

"What do they think of you being a world-famous artist?"

"I don't think they think much of it at all," he answered. "It took a few years before they even understood why I wanted to go to art school instead of a regular college, or instead of skipping college and going to work. Stephanie helped me convince them. She was always on my side, and they adored her, so it all worked out."

"She must have really believed in you."

"Yeah, she could see that I was suffocating in this town, and that a future in locksmithing wasn't going to be enough for me."

"Perceptive woman." Eve couldn't imagine anyone not seeing the potential in the man sitting across from her.

"She was always looking out for Will and me, even though I'm older. She was always looking out for everyone else. So when she got sick, it didn't occur to her to worry us with the details. At least, she had Mom and Dad and Will here when she died. I wouldn't have been able to bear it if she'd been alone."

"I know." She felt Hudson's eyes on her, but she kept hers on her wine glass, smiling sadly. "She chose to leave you out of her battle for her own reasons. She must have loved you very much."

"Yeah, I think she did. I hope she knew how much I loved her."

"I'm sure she did. You're her brother."

"You're his daughter. He knew you loved him, too."

Eve couldn't help the tears that fell. Hudson was at her side, again, helping her to wipe them away. She was amazed at the depth of tenderness in her chest that welled up whenever Hudson was near. A lake of emotion had been resting placidly inside of her, waiting for him to come along and jump in, making waves and ripples and splashing all these feelings around and over the edge.

He was a solid mass of muscle and heat next to her; she was fragile, swimming in his plaid bathrobe, the extra glass of wine making her weepy. It would have been so easy for her to turn into him, to beg him to kiss her and take her mind away from all the turmoil and angst.

Instead, she got to her feet, wiping her tears dry. She picked up her glass, the bottle of wine, and walked in the direction of the studio. "Bring the pizza if you're still hungry," she called over her shoulder.

Eve was a bit unsteady on her feet as she walked away from him. Taking her clothes off for the sake of art shouldn't have been a big deal. She'd seen enough nudes to know that models were rarely self-conscious, that it was a job, and the artists were mostly interested in the way the shadows fell and flesh rounded and veins showed through transparent skin. They wanted to see how hands and feet naturally articulated themselves, things you need a real live person to truly see. Artists weren't generally interested in their models sexually. That wasn't why she was doing it. Hudson had an incredible talent, and it broke her art-loving heart to think of him wasting it, letting it sit idle while masterpieces went unpainted. If she could help him move past this blocked phase and into a period of creating again, that would be something worthwhile, something in life she could be proud of. She'd be engendering artwork, not stealing it away, not putting something false in place of something real.

Still, her nerves nearly got the better of her when she reached the studio; the walls of glass would leave her exposed to the dark woods behind. Then she heard a click and the buzz of opaque electric sunshades lowering over each window. Hudson dimmed the track lights above to a soft glow. Heat rose from the slate floor tiles and he arranged some pillows on a love seat that was sitting in the middle of the room. She hadn't noticed it before. Had he brought it in for this occasion?

She looked over to Hudson, not sure how to proceed.

"We don't have to do this," he said neutrally. "Not right now. Not ever, if you don't want to. But if we do, I want you to be comfortable."

The use of the word "we", as if they were embarking on something together, gave her back her resolve. She took a large swallow of wine, set the glass and the bottle down on the drafting table, and walked over to the love seat. Using slow, deliberate movements, she pulled out the clip that was holding her hair in place at the top of her head. It came down in a tumble of black silk. She worked her fingers through it, until it hung in a soft drape far below her shoulders. She wasn't wearing makeup, but she could feel the heat in her cheeks giving them color, and at least her manicure and pedicure were still decent. This wasn't a test; she wasn't a model. Hudson had seen her practically naked before. She untied the robe, and, taking a deep breath, shrugged out of it, laying it over the back of the chair. She willed herself to breathe normally, to stay calm, to be utterly disinterested in Hudson's reaction to her. He was an artist right now, not a man.

When she went to sit down on the love seat, she looked up to him for direction. "How do you want me to...." She trailed off at the look of reverent awe on his face, and took no small measure of womanly pride in the swift certainty that he liked what he saw.

Eve relaxed then and positioned herself, reclining so her weight was evenly distributed. It could be physically tiring to hold one position, so she might as well take him at his word and be comfortable. She raised her eyebrows in silent invitation for approval.

"That's fine," he said slowly and started getting out materials.

Sitting out in the open, naked, was kind of fun. Since puberty, Eve had despaired of her body. She longed to be tall and waif-like, to be able to be a human clothes hanger, like the models that graced the covers of her magazines. She'd never grown much past five feet, and eventually she'd grown breasts, though they hadn't stopped growing when they reached a proportionate size to her diminutive frame. No, they'd kept expanding, rendering her depressingly top heavy. In Paris, she'd learned to dress and carry herself with ease and self-confidence, but she'd never really learned to love her body the way it was. The few men she'd been with had been happy enough to discover her ample bosom, but they hadn't had the experience or ability to bring her anywhere close to the kind of physical pleasure she'd read about in books and seen in movies. They'd been boys, safe and pleasant, with whom she'd been unafraid to get attached, because she wouldn't have to tell them anything true about herself.

Hudson was the first real man she'd allowed to touch her, to take an interest in her. She was baring herself to him in a way she'd never wanted to before.

Eve lay back and discovered that, while Hudson was busy selecting his tools, she had lost all of her nervousness. He, on the other hand, was taking an inordinately long time to comb through his pencils and straighten his sketchbook. She remembered that he was still getting his hand back after many months of disuse. He cleared his throat a few times. She heard the rustle of his papers and the tick of the heater.

"Hudson, look at me," she said softly.

He met her eyes.

"All of me," she commanded in a whisper.

He dragged his gaze down her body, taking inventory of every mole, every hair, every hollow and crest. She released the breath she'd been holding when she heard the first scratches of his pencil against paper. Hudson's stare grew less intense as he glanced quickly back and forth between her and the sketch. She could fully relax then, and marveled at how quickly his hand moved, how he seemed to fill a page in a few strokes and then move on to the next, and spend twice as long on that one before flipping it over to a fresh sheet.

Eve discovered something else unexpected as she lay there. She was being looked at, but she in turn could watch Hudson as carefully as she liked. She studied him, the way she had the first day they met as he worked the lock open on her front door. She hadn't been impressed by his lock-picking skills. But then she hadn't known it was a part time gig.

As rusty as Hudson may have been at drawing, she could tell this was an area in which he was in command. He'd spent hundreds of hours in a studio, drawing, painting, thinking, and it showed he felt comfortable in the setting. Even if his heart and brain didn't believe, his posture, the way his body sank onto the stool in front of the drafting table and his right leg hooked around one of the feet revealed this was all second nature. He had an extra pencil behind his ear, and his hair curled around his eyes. She wanted to brush it away for him, but kept still, though even this relatively easy pose was becoming difficult to maintain.

She didn't want to break his concentration, but she was all too aware of every itchy spot and cramped muscle in her body.

"Hudson?" His head jerked up. She gave him a small smile. "Would you mind if I moved into a different position?"

"No, no, not at all. It would be great if you wanted to change every couple of minutes. It'll help me get a well-rounded picture of you. I like to work quickly at this stage. Do whatever you want."

At first, she was hesitant, not sure what poses were *de rigueur*. After a few stilted efforts, she started doing what felt good, lifting her hands into the air, kneeling on one knee. She forgot she was naked, and there was nothing sexual about the positions she took up.

Watching Hudson was fascinating and she looked her fill. When she'd first met him, she'd instantly seen the basic male perfection that he exhibited, enough to fluster her even then. Now that she knew him, and what a generous, brave, passionate heart lay underneath all that hard muscle, she found him breathtakingly handsome.

As he worked, a groove of concentration appeared between his eyes, the dark winged brows hooding them with intense focus. His mouth alternated between a flat line and pursed open when he took a break and rested his pencil end on the cleft of his bottom lip. She'd had that mouth on hers before, and she was giddy with the anticipation of having it there again, having time to explore every curve, using her tongue to probe the soft skin at the corner where his lips met.

An hour passed, and a sheaf of sketching paper accumulated on the table. Hudson's movements were slower, more deliberate. Eve had thoroughly aroused herself purely by looking at the beautiful man.

"How long do these sessions usually last?" she asked in a stage whisper.

When he spoke, it sounded as if he was speaking in a dream,

his body there but his mind somewhere far away. "One more pose, all right?"

She nodded, and carefully positioned herself. She got up on her knees on the couch, so her back was to Hudson. She twisted her torso, so he could see her ass and the curve of her breasts in silhouette. She placed her hands on either side of her breasts, cupping them, thrusting them out. She stared at him, parting her lips a little. She wanted to see his reaction and know that her body could both inspire him and tear him away from his flow.

Hudson turned to a fresh page and took her in. His eyes widened, his grip on the pencil tightened, then he dropped it altogether.

"I think that's enough for tonight." His voice was dark and rough with need; he was back in the present moment.

"Is it?" She squeezed her breasts together and couldn't have counted to three before Hudson was beside her, pulling her onto his lap as he sat on the love seat, taking up most of its width.

"I don't think it's nearly enough," she managed to say before his mouth crushed against hers, and she was too busy with the exquisite pleasure of getting exactly what she wanted exactly when she wanted it. He kissed her senseless. All the imagining she'd done over the past hour coalesced into a single erotic pulse in her hot, wet center that bloomed hotter and brighter with each stroke of his tongue on hers, each frantic scrape of teeth along lips, of moan meeting moan, of breath lost to the kiss.

How could she still be herself, whole and fine, instead of the puddle of need she'd melted into the moment he'd touched her? He kissed her and kissed her and kept kissing her, his hands roaming her naked body as if they needed to feel every plane that they'd drawn over the last hour. She pressed herself closer to him, but they were decidedly lopsided in terms of layers.

"Take off your clothes," she said when she could get a syllable out around kisses.

Hudson left her mouth to tear off the long-sleeve tee he wore. Her mouth felt suddenly naked, but he returned shortly, keeping the mouth-to-mouth contact as he unbuttoned his jeans, kicking them and his boxers off in a hasty motion that left them tangled on the floor. He drew her to him again.

"Wait," she said, and he immediately stopped, breathing heavily and looking almost angry.

"What, did I hurt you?" he said.

"No, no, it's not that. I want to look at you. It's only fair."

He relaxed into a crooked smile. "Look all you want, sweetheart."

He reclined back as well as he could on the small piece of furniture. He looked like a giant trying to fit onto a dollhouse's couch.

Eve pushed away and found herself perched on the very end of the cushion. He was brown all over, though a bit lighter below his hips and above his knees. He ran daily on the beach, and the summer sun had further bronzed his naturally dark coloring. Soft black hair covered a patch of his chest in a vee, and then appeared again below his navel, leading to a thatch of curls, tighter and darker than the chocolate brown hair on his head.

Her first reaction to his stiff cock, proudly standing erect, was hesitation. It had been a while since she'd been intimate with a penis, but she'd never been acquainted with one quite as long and thick. It appeared entirely too big to fit inside her. Her second reaction was keen anticipation to try it out and see.

When she glanced back up at him, Hudson's face was endearingly expectant.

"This isn't going to work."

"It's not?" He looked stricken.

"This love seat is too small. We'll break it. Might you have a bed we can use?"

He laughed, deep and rich and with a tinge of relief. "My boudoir is at your service." With that, he gathered her into his arms and they adjourned to the bedroom.

Hudson lay her down on the center of his king-sized bed with its heavy four-poster frame as if she was a delicate egg and he a mother hen protecting her from harm.

It had been so easy to get carried away in the studio, having Eve's warm, naked flesh pressed against him, filling his hands, his mouth, his every pore. He'd wanted to bury himself in her, rutting and savage until he'd owned her body and given them both as many rounds of mindless pleasure that he could manage. Given the way he was constantly aroused when he was near her, or even thought about her, he figured he could manage quite a few rounds, indeed.

She'd had to call him off of her and it had taken a supreme effort to reign in his passion and slow things down. Eve deserved to be cherished, to be made love to with tenderness and care. He'd diverted some of his sexual drive into energy carrying her through the house and up a flight of stairs. He didn't feel her weight, only the hammer of her heart in her chest and how it beat against his own. He reveled in how well she fit against him in the protective circle of his arms. He'd be happy to have her there forever.

So he was calmer when they reached the bedroom, and he was determined to take his time, to give her what she deserved.

As he stared at her perfect feminine proportions—her curved thighs parting in invitation as soon he set her down, her hair a wild tangle, her mouth puckered and red from his kisses—his cock became unbearably hard and that sheer animal drive to be inside her returned. With a vengeance.

There was nothing but Eve—no bed, no words, no tenderness—as he covered her body with his. He took her mouth with a searing kiss and found her wet opening with the tip of his cock. Driven on by that carnal passion, he thrust his tongue in her mouth as he thrust into her. He registered her body stiffening underneath his, but the sensation of tight, wet, hot flesh around him like a vise made of pure bliss overcame everything else and he started to move, and as he rocked into her, she relaxed. He kissed down the side of her neck, but found her nipples tantalizingly out of reach. He was too far gone for anything besides the rhythm of pulling his cock out and plunging it back in, her hips meeting his, her rolling motion giving as good as she got. That vague notion that she was with him, that she wanted it this way, as hard and as fast as he could give it to her, allowed him to stay with her in the moment, give her everything he had. Her fingers, hanging onto his shoulders for dear life, dug hard into his skin and her mouth opened in a perfect O as she made a keening cry that ended in his name. That's what he heard as he came, pumping his come into her with the deepest thrusts, feeling her womanly muscles convulse around him, his name on Eve's beautiful lips.

Chapter Twenty-One

"Hudson. Hudson."

He came to himself slowly. He was in his bed. Eve was there, half underneath him, smelling of sex and sticky with the evidence of their lovemaking. It all rushed back.

"Oh my god, Eve." He was appalled. He'd practically attacked her, he hadn't used a condom, and then he'd fallen asleep, probably horrifying and crushing her in the process. He sat up and removed himself from her as delicately as he could. "I'm so sorry."

She stretched as languorously as a cat awakening from an afternoon nap. "For what?"

"For, for...using you like that."

"I'd say we used each other." She was smiling. He could only stare at her. She was taking this very calmly.

"I didn't use protection, I didn't even ask you—"

"Hudson, it's okay. I'm on birth control. I knew what I was getting into." She eyed his relaxed penis and seemed to reconsider. "Well, nearly."

"Still, I—"

"Relax. Enjoy the moment. Don't you know that it's a serious aphrodisiac for a woman to find she can incite such abandon in a man like yourself?"

"Oh, really?" He liked the sound of that. He also liked the way her hair was obscuring one of her breasts while the other lay against the sheet like a glistening apple in a gift box waiting to be plucked and eaten. "What kind of man is that?"

He figured the question would keep her busy while he started nibbling on that tender offering.

"Oh, you know. Stoic with roiling passion bubbling beneath the surface. Aloof on the outside but begging for attention on the inside. Generous with everyone except himself. More handsome than any man has a right to be."

He paused on his journey to the pert rosy nipple as her words sank in. Is that what she really thought of him? How could she hold him in such regard when he'd done nothing—well, very little—to deserve it?

"Don't stop," she said on a sigh, and he was completely done in. She kept surprising him. Tonight was one revelation after another, from her tearful confessions in the car, to her bold invitation at dinner. He'd had a raging erection the entire time she was posing for him, but he'd still managed to work up a decent rendering of her gorgeous face, and some of her other parts, as well. Her fearlessness shouldn't have surprised him after what she'd shown she was capable of, but she had this unbelievably arousing combination of innocence coupled with a desire to go after what she wanted, consequences be damned.

His heart tripped when he understood that being what she wanted was more fulfilling to him than anything had been in a long time. Perhaps ever. He wanted to be there for her, he wanted *her*, but to be wanted in return just as he was made him consider that this could be love.

"I love...your nipples." That much was true. He licked and sucked the full tip of her exposed breast until she was panting again and writhing beneath him. He loved to hear the catch in her voice when she said his name, when she tried to command him, tell him what to do, but she was already too far gone to make it sound convincing.

Hudson could afford to take his time, and so he ignored her pleas for him to get on top of her, to be inside her, even though every word she spoke drove him closer and closer to the point of no return. Instead, he gathered the hair away from her other breast, bunching it in his fist, feeling its weight and softness, indulging himself by burying his nose in it and breathing in her scent. When he had that particular smell burned into his memory, he turned his attention to her breast, holding the first one lightly in his palm so it wouldn't feel left out as he licked and suckled to his heart's content.

Eve bucked and writhed in glorious response to him, and her hands roamed his back and chest, ass, and cock. He'd never be content, never have enough of her body to last him even one day without her, never have enough of her heart until she told him what he was beginning to realize was true. He loved her. The thought grew in his mind until there was room for nothing else. It pushed its way out so that every caress, every kiss, every motion was a physical manifestation of that one truth. He loved her. He loved her with his body, silently yes, but as loudly as he knew how. Perhaps if he loved her body strongly enough, well enough, she'd hear the mantra of those three words repeating themselves over and over in his mind and in his heart until she knew the truth, too.

He moved one hand away from her breasts and found her clit with his fingers. With a certain soft pressure, he discovered he could take her up and over the edge in a few strokes. He loved being able to make her feel that way so easily. Of course, she had already returned the favor to him. He knew, as his fingers strayed lower and teased the sensitive wet folds between her thighs, that if he buried his cock in her again, it wouldn't take more than a few thrusts to feel the second greatest orgasm of his life. After the one he'd had earlier tonight, of course.

Eve's cry entered his consciousness. "Please." The single word was all the invitation he needed. He slid himself inside her, in one long fluid motion that left him buried fully in her welcoming wet flesh. There had never been so much need, so much give and take, so much pleasure. The simple act of making love would never be simple again. Love was growing with each wave of ecstasy and he couldn't, wouldn't, stop.

He came with an involuntary shudder and a cry. "Eve, I—" but she covered his mouth with a kiss before he could finish the thought.

Hudson rolled off of her, but held her close. He didn't need to say the words yet. He needed her with him, completing him in a way he hardly knew he'd been incomplete. Just as she'd disarmed his defenses, she'd reinvigorated his creativity, reminded him what was good about his art.

"I want you to know," he started, and felt her tense. It stung, but he plowed on. "How much I needed what you did for me tonight."

"The orgasms? Any time." She grinned. He loved this rare playful side of her.

"I meant posing for me. Getting me back to work. I don't want to jinx it, but I can feel things changing. I think I'm ready to work again. I can see myself focusing on people, on portraits, making a change from my old stuff."

"Really? That's fantastic!"

The enthusiasm in her voice calmed his insecure artist's brain. "Do you think so?" Eve was an undisputed authority on art. Her opinion mattered to him.

"Hudson, you have so much left to share with the world. I'm honored that you drew me. I'd be thrilled if you wanted to paint me. I think I could get over the embarrassment of being naked for the entire world to see."

He stopped her. "We'll see, but I think I'd like to keep naked Eve all to myself. Let the world see your gorgeous face. That's all they'll be able to handle."

She laughed and her cheeks turned a charming shade of pink. He liked complimenting her to the point of embarrassment. She deserved nothing less.

"I think it's a brilliant idea to start doing portraits. You'll be magnificent at it. I can't wait to see what you come out with. As long as you promise me you won't do this with your other models." She wiggled her ass against his cock, and kissed the side of his neck.

"Absolutely not," he growled. "Since I'm the only one who sees you naked. Deal?"

"Deal."

It wasn't "I love you," but he'd managed to get exclusivity into their arrangement. Progress.

ଔ

Gray light at the edge of the curtains alerted Eve to the dawn. She'd never dreaded a morning quite the way she dreaded this one. She'd stayed awake after the third incredible round of sex. She could see in Hudson's eyes that it had gone beyond sex for him, but for her to call it anything else would make it too difficult to leave. And leave she must.

If they were going to have any hope of a future together, if they were going to be able to take this seed of passion and nurture it into a fully grown relationship, then she had to make peace with the past that had been haunting her ever since she'd set foot back on American soil. Hell, if she were honest with herself, her past had been haunting every decision she'd made for the past decade.

She'd grown too fond of Hudson to continue with whatever this was and drag him into the mess that was her life even further. He'd only recently started painting again. He needed to focus on that right now. When she got her shit together, she'd come back and maybe they could try to make it work.

So she'd lain awake, reliving every moment of his body on hers, remembering the most powerful orgasms of her life, imprinting them on her memory so she'd have something to remind her that things could be good again. She lay there, feeling the rise and fall of Hudson's chest as he slept like a rock next to her, allowing herself the comfort of feeling his strong forearm around her belly, of letting his chest be her pillow, of breathing in his spicy scent with every breath. She would have been content if that was the only thing she ever smelled again.

Eve did what she did best—made a plan. She'd leave Chelsea, go to San Francisco, and finally open the manila envelope that held the details of her father's will, his legacy to her, the trust, everything. She'd find a way to forgive herself for her father's death. If she could do that, then she would deserve whatever love Hudson could give her.

She was girding herself to extricate her body from Hudson's embrace when he stirred next to her and his arms steeled, as if even in his sleep he wouldn't let her go. She traced the knuckles on the back of his hand, marveling at how beautiful, how strong and sure they were, whether they were picking a lock, drawing a face, or touching her in the most intimate of ways.

Hudson was a beautiful person, inside and out. She'd sensed it when they first met, and every action he'd made since had shown her, bit by bit, what a fine man he was. He made her feel clean and whole.

He'd shown her so much generosity, brought her so much pleasure. Eve tried to imagine what he was getting in return. A solution to his artist's block? A willing bedmate? She hoped that she'd been able to provide him pleasure in return. He'd certainly seemed aroused to the point of distraction. It had been incredibly erotic to see him lose control because of her, because of how much he wanted her. She'd met him with equal fervor, marveling at how in sync they were, how everything he did to her made her feel incredible and vice versa.

She didn't have much experience but the kind of passion they'd shared was rare and often burned out quickly. He probably reacted that way to all of his models, then burned through them like a match on a day-old newspaper. She belatedly remembered that until recently, he'd been an abstract artist who hadn't worked with models. The thought cheered her considerably. The idea of him unleashing that powerful physicality on any other woman made her heart ache.

Her exploration continued up his arm, across his powerful

shoulder, up his neck, to the surge of his pulse. He was so vital, so alive and present, bright and warm, not like the men she'd known in Europe at all. He practically radiated sunlight; he'd grown strong on this California sun. He probably drank a gallon of milk a day when he was a boy.

As she continued to probe with her fingers, she started to feel another part of his anatomy waking up. His stamina was impressive. She should really go before he woke up. But her touch was on his lips, and before she knew it, his eyes were open and he was sucking on her index finger, while his erection pressed itself with intent against her hip. She let him tease her for a moment, but resisted when he moved to roll her to her back and cover his body with hers.

She pushed him back into the mattress, and knelt over him, taking his cock in her mouth in one motion before he could protest. He called her name weakly at first, then with more strength as she managed to fit more and more of him inside her.

Eve relished the slick hardness of him, feeling supremely female as she tasted him, teased him, brought him to the edge. She would have gladly kept sucking until he came again, but he wrenched himself free, and took her mouth in such a fierce, possessive kiss that she almost came herself. She could tell the signs by now, that he was close to losing his control again, and she ran a fingernail along the underside of his cock, stroking the velvety tip, to ensure that he did. With a growl, he flipped her onto her back, and plunged into her again. They both erupted with breathless cries at the same moment.

Eve was wrung out. She was only dimly aware of Hudson withdrawing, covering her with a sheet, nestling her against him once again. He was murmuring to her, something about supper at Honeydale Farm. She was too limp to respond, too tired to tell him that she wouldn't be around for supper. She felt herself drifting into a sweet, sated sleep, as if from far away.

ଓଃ

When she awoke, the sun was high in the sky and doing its best to seep around the edges of Hudson's dark blue linen curtains. Curtains. Huh. They suited the room, with its dark wood furniture and spare lines, but they smacked of a woman's touch. His mother? Eve doubted he'd let a girlfriend give him decorating advice. Perhaps he'd hired a professional.

With a start, she realized she had been daydreaming about curtains when she had a plan to put in motion. Sleeping in was not step one of that plan.

She was alone in the bed, alone and naked and sticky from head to toe after their sex marathon. Hudson would not begrudge her a shower, though she had a pang of guilt about continuing to impose on his hospitality when she had every intention of walking out of there today without saying goodbye.

Any feeling of guilt washed away in the extra large, modern shower with its glass doors and three strategically placed showerheads. If there had been coffee waiting for her downstairs when she carried her suitcase down with her, she might seriously have considered never leaving again.

The kitchen was empty. There was only one place Hudson could be. She set a note on the kitchen counter, and picked up the Lotus keys from the table. She hesitated for a moment, caught between walking outside and heading back for the studio. She promised herself she would see him again, in time. She could do this; she could leave without saying goodbye.

Shouldering the suitcase, she went for the front door. If she'd paused to peek into the studio, it would have been that much harder for her to leave.

Chapter Twenty-Two

Hudson rotated his neck from side to side, barely noticing the pops of the vertebrae as they snapped back into alignment. He squinted at the digital clock in the corner. After one p.m.? That couldn't be right. He'd forgotten how completely zoned in on work he could be when he found his flow. Eve had done that for him, turned on a faucet of ideas and inspiration that he'd thought shut off for good.

He rubbed a hand over his stubbly chin. This was how he repaid her, by abandoning her after the most incredible night of lovemaking he'd ever experienced, followed by the most incredible morning of lovemaking.

If he had anything to say about it, the most incredible afternoon of lovemaking was shortly to begin.

First, he carefully set the watercolor to finish drying on an easel. He shuffled through the sketches he'd made last night and this morning and set a few out on the table, to remind him of the direction he wanted to go in when he next picked it up. He studied the watercolor. Eve's face stared back at him, her eyes vividly rendered, her mouth a lush paradise. Everything else was a vague impression, the slash of dark hair, the delicate pointed chin, the shell of her ear. He wanted to paint her in oils, but he needed to practice in a faster medium. It seemed like forever and like no time at all since he'd last spent a session hunched over the desk in his studio. He'd had to intentionally focus the motions of his hand at first, until they loosened up and started becoming an extension of his artist's brain.

His mind, body, and spirit were whole for the first time in a long time. He couldn't wait to share his breakthrough with the woman he loved.

He hoped she was taking a luxurious bath or, better yet, still asleep. Neither of them had slept much the night before, and he had serious plans for the rest of the day—plans that included the shower, the bed, and the shower again. However, a cup of coffee wouldn't be remiss, even that God-awful emergency instant kind. He went to the kitchen, hoping Eve wouldn't mind leftover pizza for lunch. If they were ambitious, they could go out for dinner, or maybe stay in and order Chinese. He was so high on art and sex that coffee and food battled for a distant third place in his hierarchy of needs.

He opened the cupboard and reached for the jar of coffee crystals, but his attention snagged on the note lying directly beneath on the counter. Hudson recognized Eve's bold cursive in his name on the front. Something was very wrong.

ଓ

Something was wrong. Eve had unthinkingly gotten out of the Lotus once she'd parked in front of her house. She was surprisingly happy to see it, experiencing a foreign sensation: the feeling of returning home.

She'd stopped to fill the car with gas on the way from Hudson's. She didn't think he would come after her, but she still only wanted to grab a few things and then head up north. She could be in San Francisco in three hours, return this silly car, and get her relatively practical sedan back. She'd already called to confirm reservations for Genevieve Walker at the Huntington Hotel.

But she hesitated, staring at her house. Everything looked fine in the midday sun. No alarms seemed to have been set off, all the doors and windows were closed. But again, she saw an unmistakable flash of movement in an upstairs window that was only partially covered by a curtain.

Someone was in her house.

She was parked in plain view outside. The intruder would know she was here. She saw no other vehicle, but there could have been one parked at the cul de sac around the next bend in the road.

Eve thought quickly. If the alarms had been activated, Will or the police would arrive eventually. If John or Deacon were inside, then having the police involved could get messy.

On the other hand, if she was a victim of a crime of opportunity, then the presence of Will or the police would be comforting.

The question was, would Deacon or John have even tripped the alarm?

She sat back down on the driver's seat of her car and picked her cell phone up from the center console. She scrolled down to Will's number and held her breath for four rings, about to give up when his voice came on the line.

"What can I do for you, Eve?" he said, sounding calm and strong, and enough like his brother to make her heart twinge a little. He also sounded a bit surprised. Which meant the alarm hadn't been tripped.

"Um, hi Will. Yeah, I was wondering if...I wanted to let you know that I'll be leaving town for a little while. So if you see the house dark, don't worry."

"A little while?" he asked.

"At least a week. I'll let you know if it's going to be longer than that."

"All right."

Eve resolved to go investigate when the front door opened a fraction. She heard Will as if from a distance. "...everything okay? Is Hudson giving you trouble, because if he is, I can kick his ass for you."

She swallowed around the lump in her throat. "No,

everything's fine," she said as convincingly as she could. "Thanks for the offer. I have to go now. Thanks again, Will." She ended the call.

While she'd sat in the car, the summer sun had rapidly heated the interior. She was sticky and sweaty, but she paused to gather her revolver and her keys. Even though it had to be in the low eighties, the outside air felt cool on her overheated skin. She should have been at the beach enjoying a stiff breeze and a paperback novel on this perfect, cloudless day instead of approaching her own home with a gun and a sick feeling of dread in her stomach.

Her silk blouse clung to the small of her back. She hovered on the threshold of the front door to remove her sunglasses and wipe her hands on her cotton shorts. Sweaty palms and handguns didn't mix.

She'd lived in this house for mere weeks, and she'd been away from it for a little over two days, but she hadn't recognized how much she'd come to consider it home until she walked in, breathed in the familiar scented air, saw the furniture she'd chosen herself, glimpsed the brand new deck out the kitchen's French doors as she swept through, looking for the trespasser. Home. If she left, would she ever come back?

The floor appeared to be empty, then she heard footsteps coming down the stairs. She whipped around and put her gun-wielding hand behind her back in time to see John carrying something rectangular wrapped in the white eyelet coverlet from her bed.

Three rectangular objects wrapped in various pieces from her linen closet leaned against the wall behind the front door.

She'd thought that after yesterday's betrayal she couldn't have been surprised by anything this man did, but her heart broke again, perhaps all the way through this time.

A brief flash of anger surged and then faded away until all she felt was a kind of resignation. "Don't forget the Rembrandt. It's in the guest bathroom upstairs."

John faced her, his face red from trucking up and down the

stairs. "I already got it."

"I don't suppose you left the Wyeth? It's one of my favorites."

"Sorry, darling. I'm not going to get a tenth of what these are worth and if I don't come through, I'm dead."

"I know," she said tiredly. "What happened to Deacon?"

"Dead, if he's lucky. Kwan saw right through his little magnanimous gesture. Stupid git. I wasn't there, but I know they found the Mondrian because I barely missed Kwan's goons in the hotel. Deacon must have been persuaded to tell them where to find it."

Eve was relieved that Deacon was unlikely to be a further threat, and that the painting being a fake had apparently escaped notice.

"Where are you going to sell them?" she asked, gesturing to the pile of treasures wrapped in blue polka dot sheets.

"I'm meeting a contact of Maurice's in San Francisco tomorrow. I could probably get more in New York, but I don't have the time."

"What happened?" she asked. "Why now? What did you do? What happened to everything you made over the last ten years?"

"Evie, darling, you have one of the steadiest hands in the business, you know art, but you don't have the soul of a criminal. That's probably why you managed to get out. But I have extracurricular activities that I never told you about. Somehow, my ill-gotten gains never stretched as far as I needed them to. Then I borrowed some money, quite a bit, actually, from some very unpleasant people."

"And you figured you could use me as your own personal ATM," she said, her voice betraying the barest hint of emotion.

"I'm sorry, really, I am. If I make it though this, I swear I'll make it up to you."

"You know what, John? I owed you for getting me out of the sidelines and into the game. Let's consider us even. Now, please leave my home. I meant what I said yesterday. It goes double today. I never want to see you again."

He looked vaguely confused. "You aren't going to try to stop me?"

Eve viewed the man she'd once considered a brother. "Do you want me to?"

"Evie, if I wasn't so damned desperate, you know I wouldn't do this to you."

"Then don't go back. You can go somewhere they won't find you, you can start over, like I am."

"Right," he whined. "Look how well that's working out for you."

Maybe she was naïve, but she refused to think that this was John's only option.

John seemed to consider her words, but drew up. "No. I'm sorry, but no. This is the only way. I'm going to retrieve my car from down the lane, finish loading these beauties in, and then I'll be going."

Regret seeped through her over the loss of her friend and her exquisite paintings. She was sad that these gems would disappear, go underground, in all likelihood become collateral for crimes like drug deals and money laundering. She could live with probably never seeing them again. It would be more of a crime if they were damaged or destroyed. She'd tried so hard to make amends for her sins, and it seemed that her past would never let that happen.

She nodded once, a lump in her throat. John wasted no more time on conversation. He grabbed one of the paintings in his other hand, but froze before swinging the front door all the way open.

"Who's that? Did you call the police?"

A truck cruised by her house at a crawl. Her heart leapt into her throat, but it wasn't Hudson's vehicle. Then she saw the three A's emblazoned on the side of the door. Will Cleary stopped the truck across the street, and she watched, her sense of dread growing, as he exited the cab and surveyed her house, a hand on his belt, hovering near the cell phone he kept clipped to his hip.

"Eve, I don't like this."

The note of desperation in John's voice jump-started the adrenaline pumping in her veins. He lowered the paintings to the floor and pulled a small pistol out of a holster strapped to his ankle. Deacon must have armed him.

"John." She struggled to keep her voice even and calm. "Don't worry, he's one of my contractors. I'll get rid of him and you can leave."

"He looks suspicious. Why does he look suspicious?" His hold on the gun tightened.

"He's not suspicious. Let me go out there and talk to him." She tried to tuck her gun into the waistband of her shorts and beneath her loose blouse unobtrusively so she could walk by John with it concealed.

"I don't know," he said, his voice getting tighter and tighter. Eve wondered if he was using drugs of some kind.

She'd tried calm, so she tried commanding. "John! Pull yourself together. I'll make him leave. You stay here."

He seemed to respond a bit better to her authoritative tone, but she'd lost her window of opportunity. Will tapped on the partially open front door, and John's shred of control vanished.

"Eve? Are you all right?" Will said as John yanked the door open and dragged the man inside. Eve watched helplessly as John slammed the door shut and leveled his gun at Will.

"What the hell?" Will said, surprised and then wary.

She tamped down her anger at John for putting her in this position. What mattered was getting Will out of here unharmed.

She had two aces up her sleeve—her gun, and the fact that John didn't know that Will was a security man. If he found that out, there was no telling what his paranoia might lead to.

"Will, it's all right. This is a friend of mine. He's a little nervous because he's taking these paintings to the framer for me and they're worth a lot of money. He's taking his charge very seriously."

Will looked far from convinced, and John frowned. She tried to keep her voice light. "Put away the gun, John, I'll help you load up the Lotus. You can take it and I'll take your car. Deal?"

She moved two steps toward the door, between John and Will, in the hopes that she could usher Will back outside and get him out of there without arousing his suspicions even more than they were already.

"Eve," John said in a dangerously sharp tone. She'd heard only him snap like that once before, when he had been dealing with a fence who'd gone back on his word about something. He'd ordered her to leave in that same scary voice and they'd never worked with that fence again. If she hadn't been so sheltered, she would have learned the truth about what John had done to him, understood what he was capable of. Will Cleary wouldn't be in danger because of her.

She started to turn, slowly, but John stopped her with a hand on her hip. He grabbed her gun from behind her back. She let him. She had no other choice when his gun was trained on her at close range.

"What's this?" he said, more softly, but the danger hadn't passed.

Will was keeping blessedly silent though Eve could feel the tension radiating off of him. She thought of his children, of Caitlyn, Jordan, Gracie, and cursed her naiveté. In Chelsea, her friends would come because that's what people did. Anonymous city living hadn't trained her for the dangers of helpful, caring friends.

When would she stop putting the Clearys in danger? And John had both guns.

"John, don't be silly, you can—"

"Shut up! I'm thinking." His voice was staccato like gunfire.

Eve glanced at Will, hoping her expression was reassuring. He looked frozen in place.

"Give me your cell phones," John ordered. She handed hers over slowly. John tucked her gun in his waistband and took her phone, powering it down, and then motioned with the gun to Will. "Now yours."

Will was possibly in some kind of shock, because he didn't immediately comply. Eve nudged him, and he mechanically unhooked the smartphone from his belt loop and handed it to John. When John snatched it away, Will flinched, and she sensed his fear.

The downstairs powder room was right behind John. He backed up, gun never wavering from its angle straight at her heart. He dropped the phones into the open toilet bowl. "Upstairs."

Eve heard him turn the deadbolt in the front door as she slowly walked up the staircase. Will followed her and then John, with his gun, brought up the rear.

She didn't know what he had in mind for them, but he was obviously not going to trust her to let him simply leave with the paintings. She wished there was a way to convince him that violence was completely unnecessary. She'd trade this entire house to get Will Cleary far away from this mess.

"To the guest bathroom," John said when they reached the landing.

Eve led the way. He'd chosen the only room upstairs without a window. She fervently prayed he was selecting a location to keep them sequestered while he made his getaway, and not for an out-of-the-way place to contain their bodies.

"I'll be back," he said, pushing them inside. There was no lock on the door, but the heavy leather armchair on the other side of the door would make a fine barricade for the moment.

"What the hell is going on?" Will found his voice once John was gone.

"I'm so sorry, Will. I didn't want anybody involved in this mess."

"What mess, exactly?"

"The less you know, the better, honestly."

"I presume he's the reason you wanted the security system in the first place," Will said wryly.

"Well, not him, precisely, but I had an inkling that what I had here would be tempting for someone one of these days." She caught sight of the blank space of wall where her Rembrandt had formerly hung and sighed. "Unfortunately, John taught me everything I know about disabling security systems. So he probably broke through our first two layers of security."

"What about the third?"

Chapter Twenty-Three

Snatches of Eve's letter were replaying themselves on a loop in Hudson's brain.

It's better this way. I'll call you when I figure some things out. I don't want to hurt you.

Well, she'd failed on that last count. It hurt to know they could share so much joy, happiness, even tears, and she could get up from his bed and walk away. He would have felt sorry for Eve, unable to allow herself a moment of happiness without dragging all the guilt over her father and her various sins into it, if he hadn't been so angry.

She might have been trying to pretend that she was leaving him temporarily, but what she was really doing was giving up. He knew about giving up. He'd given up who he was for two years because he thought he deserved it, he thought that denying himself his basic essence would make him feel better about his sister dying and him not being there for her. Well, now he knew that it didn't. It changed nothing. It didn't make anything better. He'd finally woken up and fully grasped that painting was his life's purpose, and he was damn sure he wasn't going to give up a second time. If he was certain about that, he was equally convinced that Eve was his other great passion.

If she had a problem with that, if she thought she could cut him out, then she was wrong.

He was going to stop her from taking off to who knew where, because he knew in his heart that if she left Chelsea today, she wouldn't ever come back and he'd never see her again.

That would not happen.

So his anger receded into a kind of fierce determination as his truck climbed the hill. He was itching for a fight that would end in glorious make up sex and then he'd put a metaphorical ring on her finger if he had to, if it would keep her close to him. That was the only option.

He frowned as he drove up to Eve's house. It seemed she had company. The Lotus and a fairly beat up black Mercedes sedan behind it took up the driveway spots. His brother's truck was parked across the street. Curious. His adrenaline, which had been calming down slowly, kicked back up. There was something off here. He passed the house, drove to the trailhead cul de sac around the bend in the road, and killed his engine. He dialed his brother's cell phone. It went straight to voicemail. That was enough to push him from concerned to worried.

He approached the house on foot through the copse of trees. He stopped stock-still in place when a figure came out of the house. He recognized John instantly, as well as the covered item he was placing in the Mercedes trunk as a painting. He also identified the bulge at John's waist. A gun. There was no sign of Will or Eve. Ice water ran in his veins. What had that bastard done with them?

John returned to the house. Eve and Will were probably inside. Hudson could call the police, but it would take too long for anyone to get here and he didn't have time to wait around for a county sheriff to show up.

The second John shut the door behind him, Hudson ran up to the front of the house, tested the door. Locked. Moving quickly, he ran to the Triple A truck, opened the cab with his spare key, and grabbed a few items from the toolbox on the floor of the passenger seat.

He palmed a crowbar and a lock pick set and raced to the

front door. Eve and Will had done a first rate job of securing the house against the casual intruder. He had picked this lock once before, but that had been a flimsy hardware store lock. Now it had a sturdy deadbolt, but he had to believe he could do it. He couldn't risk the noise of breaking a window.

If John came out of the door while he was working on it, then that's where the crowbar came in.

One long minute passed. Hudson didn't hear anything inside. No talking, no footsteps. No gunshots. He had to be thankful for that, at least.

Time stood still as he struggled with the lock. He remembered the lock cutting device that was surely somewhere in the truck, but it was too late to go back and look for it.

The sweat dripped off his forehead when the lock finally tumbled open. He turned the doorknob slowly, silently, and gripped the crowbar with a hand that was trembling with the fine motor exertion of lock picking.

☙

"How you holding up, Will?"

Will was sitting on the floor, his head resting on the tops of his drawn-up knees.

"I can't believe I stood there while that jerk pointed a gun at you."

"You did the right thing," she said. "I've known John for ten years, but I've never seen him this way. He's desperate, which makes him unpredictable. I still don't think he'll hurt us. I already gave him my blessing to take the paintings. He has to believe that we aren't going to call the police the moment he's gone."

"But he's stealing your stuff!"

"That's not important. What's important is that when he leaves, he leaves us intact." She paused. "What's that?" She heard a clatter of footsteps and the thud as the armchair was wrenched away from the door. John stood in the doorway, looking wild-eyed.

"Who's here, what have you done?" he hissed.

"What you talking about?"

He waved the gun around. Eve forced herself not to cringe when it floated in her direction. "The front door is open! What's going on? I swear to God, Eve," John yelled. The gun was pointed straight at her.

For the first time that day, Eve was stopped cold in true fear. She wished she could have seen Hudson one more time, taken back that ridiculous note, clung to him with her entire being. She hoped there would be time for that. "I have no idea what—"

A crunch, a thump, and a rattle followed one another in quick succession. John crumpled to the floor; the gun skittered across the bathroom to land at Eve's feet. She scooped it up, and rose to come face to face with a heavily breathing, crowbar-wielding Hudson. She looked from Hudson to John and back again.

"Excellent timing," she said.

Hudson looked at her and dropped the crowbar at his feet. "Are you all right?"

She smiled and her shoulders drooped in relief. "We're fine. Where did you come from?"

"I'll tell you in a minute. What are we going to do with this asshole?"

Eve considered. "I guess we should wait for the police to get here and tell them what happened."

"The police?"

"They should be on their way. John disabled my alarm system, but he didn't know that I have an emergency button on my key fob." She held up her key ring, with its whimsical Eiffel Tower key chain. Hudson could see a discrete button attached to its base.

"When it looked like John couldn't be trusted to leave us alone, I pressed it. It's attached to my security contract with the city, so they dispatch a car. It should arrive within thirty minutes." As she spoke, she took possession of her gun and made sure the safety was on before tucking it back in her waistband. John's gun was emptied of bullets and placed carefully on the bathroom counter.

"You rigged this up for her?" Hudson asked Will.

"She asked me to come up with a fail safe. There are a couple more buttons hidden through the house."

"Now let's get our story straight before the police arrive," she said. "Will, all you need to know is what you saw. Hudson and I should probably talk a little. Do you want to wait downstairs? If John didn't do something to it, you can use my landline to call the cops, make sure they are on their way. Tell them to send an ambulance, too."

Will shrugged. "I don't want to know anything. I'm glad you showed up when you did, bro." They gave each other an awkward man-hug and Will practically ran downstairs, away from the unconscious man on the floor.

Eve repressed a wave of nausea as she inspected the bloody gash on the side of John's head. "He's not going anywhere. Do you think we could sit down?"

Hudson took her arm and led her to the guest bed, which had been stripped to the fitted sheet to make painting wrappings. She sank down on the mattress, stiff in his arms.

She'd never felt so self-conscious. She'd run out on him and he'd saved her life. "You must be mad at me," she said, her face turned to his flannel-covered chest. Her voice was small. She'd faced down a gun-toting maniac but couldn't meet Hudson's eyes.

His arms tightened around her, his face buried in her hair. "I'm furious with you," he whispered. He kissed the top of her head. "But I think I'll get over it."

Eve risked a glance at him. He rained kisses down on her forehead, her cheeks, and then put one kiss, soft as a brush from an apple blossom, on her lips.

She could float away on that kiss and never come back down to Earth.

Then a distant voice called, "They're on their way!" and the moment was broken.

"Um, we really do need to get our story straight," she said mournfully.

"Okay. What happened?"

"I think we can tell them the truth. John was an old friend. He came to the States, and knew I was out of town, so he tried to rob me of my paintings, for which I have legitimate proof of ownership. I came home early, caught him in the act. Your brother happened to be in the neighborhood and came by to check on things. John locked us up in the bathroom and would have done God knows what if you hadn't come along and clocked him."

"So no mention of Deacon, Mondrians, or any other art thefts?"

"I highly doubt John will be bringing that up, so I don't see any reason to mention it."

"Fine by me."

"We can omit the part about my gun, I think. I don't technically have a license for it."

"Do you want to go mention that to Will? I'll stay here with John."

"You aren't going to hurt him more, are you?" she asked, only half in jest.

"I don't kick a man when he's down, but I'd like to kill him for what he did to you, what he tried to do to you. Not to mention taking your paintings."

"I'm almost sorry he didn't get away. I suppose the men he's afraid of can get to him in prison."

"Eve, that's not your problem. He tried to hurt you. He could have killed you, and my brother. I'm not exactly a fan."

A wail could be heard as emergency vehicles climbed the hill.

Eve rose to leave and face the sordid business ahead.

"One more thing, Eve. We're not finished." His expression was unreadable but she could sense the threat, and the promise, of those words.

She nodded, once, then turned and fled.

Chapter Twenty-Four

Eve was alone. The house had grown two sizes smaller while the EMTs trudged through with their equipment, and the sheriff arrived, and then another squad car and a unit with cameras and evidence collecting equipment. It had been near chaos for a while, people taking statements and photographs. One by one, each of the unwelcome visitors left.

First John had gone, handcuffed to the stretcher, his head wrapped in a bandage, an IV flowing into his arm. He was conscious but woozy. His prognosis was likely a full recovery after some MRIs and other diagnostic procedures. Eve followed him out, dismayed to see someone she'd once been close to hurt, but she couldn't regret her actions or Hudson's. She didn't know if she'd get a say in the charges against him, but she'd already made up her mind to pay for his defense and maybe even to square him with the villains he owed money to. It felt like the right thing to do.

After all, she had her paintings back. They'd been tagged for evidence, but she'd convinced the officers not to cart them away after they'd been photographed. She sensed they'd been nervous about transporting such valuable pieces, and they'd relented with a warning not to do anything with them until the case was closed.

Then Will had gone home to Nancine and the kids, shrugging off Eve's endless apologies. "It comes with the territory, I guess. You are my most high profile client."

"Well, consider a bonus for combat duty coming your way," she said with a smile.

He shook his head. "Be good to Hudson. He looks like Hell. That's enough for me."

She nodded and her heart twisted. She didn't know how well she'd done in that department so far.

Hudson bore the bulk of the police scrutiny. His fingerprints had been taken and he'd been questioned thoroughly about his reasons for entering the house and hitting John in the head with an iron bar. He explained how his suspicions were aroused and he'd brought the crowbar along in case he couldn't get the front door open any other way, but then used it to subdue the gun-toting intruder. Eve wasn't worried as anyone could see he'd acted in self-defense and to rescue her and Will. Hudson was well known in the community both as an artist and as an activist and volunteer. She supposed the police had to cross all their Ts.

The deputy had asked him to come to the station for a few more rounds of paperwork, so he'd said a brief and serious goodbye. A tow truck came and impounded the Mercedes that John had acquired along the way. Eve was well and truly alone, and the house felt big and empty.

Hudson's last words to her seemed to be bouncing off the quiet walls and around her brain. She was tempted to get in the car and drive away from her house, from John, and from Hudson, too. She could pretend it would never have worked out, that they weren't meant to be. But she'd be lying. Hudson wouldn't let her go. The knowledge that he'd come that day to prevent her from leaving and had stopped her from being hurt or killed instead gave her the strength to stay where she was.

It had been a lifetime since she'd woken up in Hudson's bed that morning, but evening had barely fallen. Her stomach growled urgently, calling for dinner. Food had been forgotten in the day's events.

She didn't have to look to know her cupboards were bare. Trekking into town for groceries or take out seemed to require more energy than she could muster.

Then she remembered. Sunday Supper at Honeydale Farm.

Rue was warmly enthusiastic when Eve called to invite herself over. She showered and changed and found an offering—a bottle of champagne, of course. Before she left, she used her landline to leave a message on Hudson's cell to meet her if he was able. She kept the message neutral, but he'd realize what she meant by accepting his earlier invitation, in a roundabout way.

The heat from the day had mellowed into a warm summer's evening. Dusk darkened the woods and kept the sky clear and bright, so she decided to walk down the hill. It felt scandalously good to move around in the fresh air, having stepped off the emotional roller coaster of the past few days. She felt like skipping, something she hadn't done since childhood. If the bottle of champagne wouldn't have been the worse for it, she might have broken out into a skip, but she did have her priorities.

Everything she'd written in that note to Hudson had been wrong. She did need to go and face her father's legacy, but she could do it with Hudson at her side. He needed room to rediscover himself as an artist, but he could do it with her cheering him on. There was no need to compartmentalize her life simply because that's what she'd done in the past.

Eve finally understood what made Hudson such an innately generous man. He shared himself with her, he shared his life with her, and when she'd had a problem, he'd shared that as well. He wouldn't see her problems as deal breakers; he'd see them as challenges that could be overcome more easily by two than by one. It felt so good to know she didn't have to do everything alone anymore. She forgot about the champagne as she dashed down the last bit of the hill that led to the farm's gravel driveway. She wanted to tell Hudson as soon as she humanly could. She didn't have a cell phone, but she'd borrow Rue's and she'd call him and call him until he came to her. Or she'd borrow a vehicle from Rue and go to him. Whatever it took. She didn't want to wait anymore to have what she'd always wanted. Home. Family. Love.

Hudson was standing on the front porch of the farmhouse when she ran up. He was dressed exactly as she'd seen him a mere two hours before, but he looked more handsome than she'd ever imagined. Two days of beard gave him a charmingly disreputable air, his hair still needed that trim, and his shirt was wrinkled beyond hope. She beamed at him and his smile of return was the sweetest thing she'd ever seen in her life, sweeter than the Pietà or her favorite Raphael or Monet's water lilies.

She ran up the steps, nodded to Rue who was chatting with a few other guests, thrust the bottle into her hands and said, "We'll be back in a minute." She pulled Hudson down the steps, to the side of the house where Rue's vegetable garden tumbled out of its wooden enclosure. Zucchini plants and runaway tomato vines spread around them, and she didn't let go of Hudson's hands.

"I'm so happy you're here," she said. "Are you all right? They didn't give you a hard time?"

He smiled. "They were very polite. They said it all seemed very straightforward and that they'd be in touch if they needed more information. I'm not in trouble or anything."

"Thank God. What a mess. I cannot wait to have that behind us."

"Behind us?" he said. "You mean, there's an us?"

"I'd like there to be," she said, suddenly shy. "I know I behaved terribly. I ran away because I thought I needed to be alone to straighten out my life. I am tired of being alone. Now that I've met you, I know that I wouldn't be alone even if I was alone, because you'd be there with me, in my head, in my heart. If you're always with me there, then I want you by my side as well."

"You do?" Hudson pretended to disbelieve.

"Yes, you vexing man! I do. Are you going to make me say it first?"

"I think so."

"All right...." She took a deep breath. "I love you. I'm in love with you, Hudson Cleary."

"I love you too, Eve Caplin," he said right on her heels, putting her out of her misery.

"Wait, there's something else you need to know about me. You're not in love with Eve Caplin."

"What do you mean?" He looked wary.

She cleared her throat. "My real name is Genevieve Walker. My father was Richmond Walker."

"Richmond Walker, of R. Walker Investments? With the ads starring the talking dog?" Hudson looked adorably confused.

"I'm afraid so. Also, I turned twenty eight two months ago."

Hudson's brow furrows deepened even more. "So?"

"So my inheritance was held in trust until my twenty-eighth birthday. I'm a very wealthy woman." Her voice was apologetic.

"You own a Cézanne and a Rembrandt. I think I already knew you had money."

"Those are ill gotten gains. I'm even thinking about donating them to a museum and washing my hands clean. I'm talking about my father's legacy. I'm a part owner of the business and there are the houses and investments and some other things. I thought I didn't want the responsibility. I thought I could come here and pretend all of that didn't exist. Knowing you has shown me I can't brush it under the rug. If you'll stay with me, then I know I'll have the strength to deal with it all. I already have some ideas about how to use the money to endow art scholarships in schools."

"Sweetheart, you're a natural. If you're trying to scare me off, it isn't going to work. I don't care what your name is, or who your father was, or how much you're worth. You're priceless to me. I'd be proud to stand by you and help you deal with whatever comes your way. In fact, I'd like to be legally bound to do so."

"What do—oh!"

Hudson was down on one knee, his hands holding hers, the sunset a pink and orange glow behind him, as if the colors of her heart were painting the sky. The air smelled like wet grass and sun-warmed tomatoes and Eve's chest was near bursting from the welling of emotion inside her.

"Genevieve Walker, aka Eve Caplin, former art thief, future philanthropist, will you allow me to love you forever and will you love me in return? Will you be my wife?"

"I will," she breathed, and he laughed and pulled her into an embrace, setting her on his knee and capturing her mouth in a kiss that sent a tingle of electricity straight to her heart.

She couldn't imagine loving a man more than she did at that moment, but each day together would grow and strengthen their love for one another. Life with Hudson was a journey she couldn't wait to take.

~ABOUT THE AUTHOR~

Libby Waterford writes California-set steamy contemporary romances. She lives in Los Angeles with her family and works off her weekly pilgrimage to In-N-Out by swimming and climbing the city's hidden staircases.

You can visit Libby at:
www.libbywaterford.com

Made in the USA
Middletown, DE
23 August 2020